Strangers

Strangers

by Barbara Ewing

Atheneum
New York
1978

Library of Congress Cataloging in Publication Data

Ewing, Barbara
    Strangers.

    I. Title.
PZ4.E949St   1978   [PR9639.3.E92]   823   77-15348
ISBN 0 - 689-10855 - 9

*to Anne Darnborough Page to Samoo Pillay and
to the old Maungatapu Maori Primary School*

Strangers

Chapter I

Lots of people were drunk and they kept throwing coloured toilet rolls up on the deck from the wharf and singing 'Waltzing Matilda' very loudly and some people were crying. I leaned on the rail where there was a space and waved to Mum and Dad and two friends from the office and the director of the local amateur theatre group and my brother. We weren't drunk, we'd had tea and pavlova cake for a goodbye afternoon tea sitting on our wooden verandah in the shade.

The sun beat down on the deck and the wharf, tar melted between old wooden boards, seagulls cried around the stern of the ship where stewards were throwing buckets of scraps and the big ropes creaked as the ship bumped gently now and then against the old tyres on the wharf-posts. Sun danced and flashed off the tin roofs of storage sheds and people shaded their eyes as they waved. The heat shimmered between me and them and there was no breeze at all and I could smell the heat and the sea and the tar and the ropes and the ship's engine. Mum was wearing a green hat and green gloves and Dad and my brother wore shorts with a shirt and tie.

Then the ship gave a long loud hoot and men unwound big ropes and threw them and slowly we pulled away from the wharf and people sang and shouted and waved and the toilet rolls and the streamers tautened and snapped and fluttered gently down into the water.

'Goodbye everybody,' I called over the ship's rail.

'*Waltzing Matilda, who'll come a-waltzing Matilda with me*,' sang the people on the wharf.

They grew smaller and smaller but for a long time I could see, shimmering in the heat like the water, Mum's green glove waving one of Dad's white handkerchiefs.

Chapter II

December in London. I saw snow falling on bananas in a street market and men with purple noses stamping their feet and digging their hands deep into their pockets. The Thames seemed very yellow and dirty after all that poetry we'd learned at school.

I had never been so cold in my life. I found a warm place for sitting: the Westminster Reference Library behind Leicester Square.

'*Goodbye Leicester Square*', my parents used to sing at parties with someone playing the piano. It seemed a rather small piece of grass to sing about.

I sat in the library at a table by the window and wrote letters home and watched the old men sniffling and snoozing over newspapers and the African students, so black, studying at every table. Quiet footsteps and lowered voices, an occasional telephone ringing and the noise of a pneumatic drill somewhere. There was an old lady who used to come every day with brown carrier bags that she used to rummage in, and the paper inside used to crackle. One day she ate a sandwich, pecking at it surreptitiously and darting her eyes about, like a bird.

I couldn't stay with my Australian friends for ever, sleeping on their floor in Tooting Bec. I found a room in Fulham which would be quite near the Institution if I got accepted. The landlady was kind and old and deaf and unmarried, she bathed on Sundays and thought the Queen was lovely. She said that if I kept insisting on having a bath every day I'd get TB and the LCC would come and take me away.

'Oh,' I said, wondering if that could be true in England because of the cold, reminding myself to ask my friends in Tooting Bec.

'You are *stupid*,' they said, and laughed.

Lots of old people lived in rooms in that street. They sat by their curtains and looked out all day and often at night too. I would see the curtains moving slightly as I walked past. It was very cold for them in the winter and some of them died.

They put up decorations in Regent Street. I walked along bumping into hurrying people and looking in shop windows. People do hurry along looking pained in London in the winter, me too I suppose, because the cold hurts so much. I'd never imagined such coldness could exist and my toothbrush froze over with ice in the Fulham house. So grey everything, and darkness beginning at three o'clock in the afternoon so that at first I thought I might be going blind. Advertisements in tube stations said have a Guinness so I looked to see how much money I had and realized I would have to get a job. Roses were three and sixpence each.

There seemed to be a lot of black people everywhere. In Australia I'd hardly noticed them, just a few Asian students in the streets and the Aborigines mostly lived a long way away somewhere. But in London there seemed to be so many. Black students in the public libraries always wearing suits and ties. Black conductors on the buses who didn't smile much and were surly to people and had pink palms. And along the part of the Fulham Road where I sometimes went shopping, black people in fantastic costumes, purples and reds and yellows that shone out in the grey streets. Once a black man tried to pick me up at Piccadilly Circus while I was looking through an 'A to Z' street guide.

'Can I help you?' he said very politely in a posh English voice. He had fuzzy hair like a pot cleaner and his white teeth shone as he smiled at me.

'No thank you,' I said and ran into the Underground where the escalators seemed to be full of people *with* each other, except for me.

I cried sometimes at the joined-together houses and the million chimney pots and the early darkness and the cold of that first winter. It was a long way from Sydney Australia and the long low wooden houses in the suburbs, and the sea.

'Get a typing job while you're waiting,' said my Australian friends in Tooting Bec, 'there's plenty of typing jobs.'

'No, I *hate* the clicking noise typewriters make in offices. I am never never, never going to type anymore, ever. I'm supposed to try and be an actress now you know, not a typist.' But there were still six weeks till the Institution auditions. Then an Australian boy I knew told me how to apply for a job at one of the lesser known English Language Schools that teach English to foreigners.

'I couldn't teach,' I said.

'Listen,' he said, '*anybody* can do that job. They give you a book and you read out of it to the pupils and you get twelve and sixpence an hour. That's *all* you do, read out of a textbook.'

'Oh,' I said.

'Go *on*,' he said.

'All right,' I said.

So I went nervously to a school in a falling-down building at the back of Oxford Street. I said, blushing, that I was a trained teacher and made up a few other qualifications but they pointed out that my Australian accent wasn't quite what was required. Luckily I left my telephone number because a few days later one of the teachers committed suicide and they needed someone in a hurry.

I had two two-hour classes a day. In the afternoon came the German and Spanish *au pair* girls, and the two Chinese waiters who had to come after lunch and before dinner when the Chinese restaurants were quiet. I think there was a ruling that foreigners could only come to live in England if they took English classes. There was a special set course leading to an examination they were supposed to sit so I read to them about the verb 'to be' from the special book provided, and they had to practise reading aloud from a simplified version of *Jane Eyre*. I was a terrible teacher. When I wasn't reading to them from the prescribed books I couldn't think of anything to say.

In the evening it was a beginners' class. Italian waitresses half collapsing with tiredness, Spanish espresso-lever-pullers who kept asking me to the pictures, and a Greek who couldn't speak any English at all. Sometimes I heard the strange Welshman who ran the place listening outside the door. I thought he would probably fire me soon. We had one single-bar electric heater in the classroom. We all wore our coats and sometimes the youngest Italian waitress who was fifteen fell asleep, pale and dark-haired, leaning against her sister's shoulder. Then we would all talk softly. The room smelt of chalk and sometimes, when I wrote something from the book on to the blackboard, I accidentally scratched my nail across it and everyone winced.

After six weeks I had passed my audition, so I left them and the strange Welshman and the one-bar heater to start classes at the Institution.

Chapter III

The Institution, one of the most famous drama schools in the world, in a side street off the King's Road in Chelsea, had the masks of Comedy and Tragedy over the entrance doors. I looked up at them as I went through the doors on the first day.

'Why don't you go to England and study at a drama school with your grandfather's money,' said the director of our amateur dramatic society.

'I couldn't be an *actress*,' I said.

'Yes,' he said, handsome and sunburnt from surfing. 'Yes, I think you could.'

I thought about it as the typewriters in the office sounded in my head.

'All right,' I said.

A man in a strange red uniform shepherded me and the

rest of my class into a room. We were given a list of things we had to get: tights, ballet shoes, a copy of *Voice and Speech in the Theatre* by J. Clifford Turner, various books on the history of the theatre, long rehearsal skirts and fans for the girls, stage make-up, bone props to hold our mouths open in speech classes. In a breathless room we listened to a speech by the principal who welcomed us.

'I hope you will be happy here. Don't ever be late for anything, that is unforgiveable. The work is hard the hours are long – look after your health.' He looked over his glasses with something that might have been interest and might have been pity at the girls sitting in front of him. He cleared his throat and then took his glasses off.

'There is something you girls should be aware of always. There are three times as many women as men trying to make a living in this profession. There are three times as many parts for men available as parts for women. That means that the men sitting beside you have nine times the chance that you have of getting work when you leave the Institution, unless you are very very talented and very very lucky. And even the men aren't going to find it easy. I tell you this now because women working in the theatre have a very difficult time and I think you should understand this right at the beginning.'

A little hesitant smile from one student to another. One or two familiar faces, students I'd seen at the nerve-racking auditions a few weeks earlier. I looked at the girls. Most of them seemed prettier than me; one I had heard already was the daughter of a famous film star. A couple of good-looking boys, some funny-looking ones. The boys were looking at us too. A scraping of chairs as the principal cleared his throat for the last time, put his glasses on again and left us. A general move to the cafeteria, we all seemed to shuffle along together, wanting reassurance from one another. Everywhere, along the corridors and up and down the stairs, we saw the real students, the ones that belonged so confidently, girls with long hair and eyes made up heavily, girls wearing no make up at all, men wearing jeans, a bald man, groups laughing and calling and pushing past us, in a hurry, doing something, going somewhere. A piano being played as we passed a room; from another, bewildering sounds of male voices sort of going ngoooo ngaaaa.

And the smell that I was to know so well for so long, a smell that permeated the whole building, a mixture of floor polish and dust and sandshoes and sometimes mingling with it faintly the smell of overcooked cabbage.

I nervously pulled on my black woollen tights in the Ladies' Locker Room for our first movement class, bumped into a girl who was crying, almost slipped on the polished floor and finally found the room I was looking for. Everyone seemed to be talking to someone so I talked to a fat little blonde girl with broken glasses who looked like Marilyn Monroe and told me that her name was Samantha and that she had been a manicurist. She also told me that the rest of our class consisted of an architectural student, a naval rating, a professional actress from California, that handsome fellow over there from Birmingham who used to be in the Army, a starlet sent by a film company ('which one?' 'that one'), the grand-nephew of the Indian Minister for Communications, two teachers, a girl from Persia, a famous film star's daughter ('which one?' 'that one,'), two boys who had just left school, and an Australian shorthand typist.

'Oh – I mean that's you,' and she giggled and pushed her broken glasses on more firmly.

'How do you *know*?' I whispered.

'I had a quick look at the records,' she whispered back.

The class started and I had to do skipping with the naval rating.

We had fencing classes and got the giggles and the man glared at us.

'Riposte! Riposte!' he shouted striding up and down the room.

Speech classes, where I found out what terrible English I spoke and the teacher sighed and asked me to do more exercises.

'Mahnahlah, maynaylay, meeneelee, maynaylay,' she said to me, over and over again.

Movement classes started off like physical education classes: jumping and skipping and running and stretching and bending. Then the teacher started saying funny things to us.

'Anthony, your bending is heavy and boring and dull, just like your jumping. Try to bend lightly and interestingly.'

'Pardon?' said Anthony, the architectural student.

'It permeates all your movement, this heaviness and

dullness. It will interfere with your work too. Try to find lightness.'

Anthony looked bewildered and mumbled into a corner with the grand-nephew of the Indian Minister for Communications.

'Alfie,' continued the teacher, 'try not to skip so aggressively.'

In the mime class I had to work in a group with the starlet sent by a film company, the Persian girl and a teacher. We had to pretend we were walking in a storm at night, trying to find shelter.

'This is stupid,' said the starlet, Jennifer-Anne, 'I didn't have to do this when I was with Gregory Peck.'

There were awful compulsory singing classes where everyone had to sing a song on their own. I sang Goodbye Piccadilly Farewell Leicester Square and the famous film star's daughter sang a song out of one of her father's films. She didn't sing very well and everyone looked embarrassed and Samantha giggled.

Anthony, the architectural student, prepared a scene from *Hamlet* for the Acting Class. It was dull and heavy and boring.

Make-up classes: shadows and highlights and Samantha staring at herself in the mirror, looking rather strange.

There were always people crying in the lavatories, sometimes pretending not to. One girl was lying on the floor weeping loudly while people stepped over her to change their shoes. 'What's the matter?' I said, bending down but she only wept louder and I wondered if she was perhaps rehearsing for something. Another girl beckoned me away and told me that the girl on the floor did this regularly and she'd stop soon.

'Oh,' I said. 'I see.'

'Open ze groin,' shouted the old French lady who taught us classical movement. 'How can you walk wiz style if you don't open ze groin. One two one two head up shoulders back feel proud open ze groin.'

'Your bending is rather naive,' said the movement teacher to me. 'Try to be more positive.'

'Oh,' I said. 'Yes.' And I bended and bended, as positively as I could.

One day the Persian girl started screaming and shouting and they took her away in an ambulance.

One day Samantha, the Marilyn Monroe one with the broken glasses started screaming and shouting too and ran crying into the locker room. It wasn't like her. She's pregnant, she's pregnant, we told one another. People tried to arrange abortions and our class whispered together on the stairs. Her former employer, the manicurist, could lend her forty pounds . . . there was a woman . . . off the Edgware Road . . .

She told her father that she was staying at my place and went off to Edgware Road. There were two tries at an abortion but nothing happened . . . she's more than three months pregnant, we told one another . . . it's too dangerous . . . One morning at a quarter to eight she rang me.

'It's all done it's finished it had it had I saw little fingers when it came out. It hurt and hurt and I had to put the gramophone on very loud so me Dad wouldn't hear me cry out.' She came to speech class that afternoon, pale, leaning against a wall slightly as she recited in her London accent:

> The Star that bids the Shepherd fold,
> Now the top of Heav'n doth hold,
> And the gilded Car of Day,
> His glowing Axle doth allay
> In the steep Atlantick stream . . .

She still hadn't had her glasses mended and made lots of mistakes.

I sat outside in the sun on the warm concrete learning a speech from *As You Like It*. Alfie came and sat beside me, the Irish factory-worker's son, the one who grew up in Birmingham and had been in the Army, the good-looking one with black hair and green eyes and the accent that was more fashionable than mine.

'Why are you nice to everyone except me?' he said aggressively.

'Am I nice to everyone except you?'

'Yes. You are.'

We went to the pub where all the students drank,

mostly half pints of bitter. We sat in a corner and talked about Life and all our Unhappy Love Affairs. I rather exaggerated my hot nights on the Sydney beaches with the waves crashing on to the sand because Alfie's stories were so amazing: seduced by a woman in a kitchen when he was thirteen and getting VD from a writer before he even went into the Army. I thought to myself that he must be making it up. He walked me home to my room in Fulham. I took my shoes off and Alfie who was a bit drunk sang an Irish song about a tinker who mended pots and pans for ladies when their husbands were out and we walked along the dirty grey streets in the summery evening knowing we were both going to be famous film stars, smiling at each other and holding hands.

The sounds of the Institution. In the morning if you got there early enough, I discovered, you could hear the cleaners singing 'I Could Have Danced All Night' as they polished the floors. Then a few students would come yawning up the stairs, shut themselves in an empty classroom, and do voice exercises:

mahnahlah, maynaylay, meeneelee, maynaylay
mahnahlah, mawnawlaw, moonooloo, mawnawlaw
mahnahlah . . .

At ten o'clock a bell would go and classes would start: a piano from the music-room or a mime class, heavy bangs from a movement class, 'Is this a dagger which I see before me?' in unison from a men's voice class, a scene from *The Rivals* and a scene from *Suddenly Last Summer* being rehearsed in adjoining rooms. 'How many eggs you want this morning luv?' someone might call up the stairs to the cafeteria. Phones rang in the offices and the traffic went past along the King's Road. All day long voices and pianos and bangs. A girl in a corridor is crying but is she unhappy or is it a scene from a play? But I don't quite like to ask anymore so I just go and change my shoes.

The daughter of the famous film star would always sit close to someone, anyone, male or female it didn't matter, someone to be close to, someone to touch, to be with. Once in a lecture she sat on the floor by my chair, she leaned against my legs and rested her head on my knee, her hand idly caressing my foot. I felt embarrassed. As I moved uncomfortably away I saw her face, hurt and longing.

The end of the first term came. We had our exams: practical examinations in front of the principal and staff. Nerve-racking mornings in stuffy classrooms. The famous film star's daughter was kicked out along with the grand-nephew of the Indian Minister for Communications and two others.

Chapter IV

At the beginning of the second term Alfie and I decided to live together. It seemed so fashionable and I thought to myself rather proudly that my bending would probably not be so naive from now on. So we had to find a place to live and I had to acquire a wedding ring and go to the Family Planning Association where they asked me how long we had been married and fitted me with things. And in Islington we found a basement flat for six pounds ten shillings per week though I can't say exactly where because we left without paying the last electricity bill. This flat had a front room that looked out on to people's legs passing: trousers and stockings and high-heeled shoes. The bedroom had two thin single beds with faded green candlewick bedspreads and a net curtain across the only window which looked out on to a grey concrete wall. The bath was in the kitchen, it had a top on it so that you could use it as a shelf when no one was having a bath. Alfie said we should get a place where we shared a bath because it would be cheaper but I wanted one of our own. The lavatory was outside, across a concrete path. Summer autumn winter spring – this flat was always dark and always cold. And I suppose there must be someone living in it right now, having the electric light on all day long and wanting the two-bar heater on all the time and worrying about how much it is costing. But on the late-summer evening when we moved in it seemed very romantic. A friend with a car had helped us move our belongings and we all went off to a pub to have a drink. Green leaves shine in London on a summer evening, a different green from Australia, the setting sun catches them somehow and they shine a golden green, even in Islington, and we held hands Alfie and I and we watched the leaves and the sky and drank half pints of bitter and talked with our friend. I remember most a feeling of sophistication. I was *living* with someone like people did, especially actresses. And so we went – home – and that night we didn't notice the cold or the darkness or the concrete wall outside the bedroom window.

Alfie, in the kitchen, kept getting angry with me.

'Clean As You Go!' he would admonish me, 'Clean As You *Go*!' and if I was cooking a meal he would move behind me wrapping up potato peelings, washing knives and throwing away packets I was using which had 'Instructions for Cooking' written on them.

'Why can't I clean up *after*?' I said.

'Clean As You Go!' he shouted, 'it's much more efficient and keeps the kitchen tidier.'

The bath caused a lot of trouble. At night or in the morning I would lie in the bath listening to the transistor radio. Alfie would get beside himself with rage.

'You're indulging yourself, you're just indulging your senses, it's unnecessary to bath the way you do.'

'But – in Australia . . .' But he would go to the Institution without me, slamming the door behind him. I would arrive late for class and mumble something to the lecturer and Alfie wouldn't look at me. Perhaps it would be the day that he and I and Anna, the professional actress from California, were supposed to work together on a mime about Children at the Seaside, or the day I had to sing 'I Feel Pretty' in the singing class, standing up there by the piano singing slightly out of tune while Alfie looked angrily out of the window.

I wore the wedding ring on my right hand in the daytime and after classes on my left. I was always changing it over in the bus or somewhere.

Alfie had been a very good footballer when he was in the army and had had his nose broken badly which affected his voice, made it very nasal. He was anxious to remedy this as well as his Birmingham accent. He was fantastically hard-working and ambitious and dedicated to the theatre and he would stay behind at the Institution after classes had finished, doing voice exercises for hours, working on scenes, doing breathing exercises. At night he would shut himself in the front room for two or three hours at a time and over and over again I would hear him:

Mahnahlah, maynaylay, meeneelee, maynaylay, mahnahlah, mawnawlaw, moonooloo, mawnawlaw.

On these long dark cold evenings I would lie in the bedroom on the pale green candlewick bedspread staring at the concrete wall wondering why Alfie had seemed so preferable to my deaf kind landlady in Fulham.

And through the wall his voice came: the nasal tone, the Birmingham accent he was trying so hard to lose.

OOSP
OHSP
AWSP
AHSP
AYSP
EESP

'Where's the brown sauce?' said Alfie, 'pass the brown sauce.'

'But – it's something special, it took ages to make, there's bits of pineapple in it, and red peppers.'

'I always have brown sauce,' said Alfie, 'and give me some bread and butter.'

In the beginning in the mornings we would wake up and be glad that there was someone to wake up beside and we would take turns to jump on to the cold floor and make the coffee and bring the mugs back to bed. The mugs were brown, brown mugs of Nescafé steaming in the cold mornings and the arms of another person and no loneliness. And I used to often think of those poor people on escalators in tubes, by themselves in a crowd of people, and be glad that I wasn't one of them any more. But it wasn't so long before we would wake in the mornings and just lie there, neither of us speaking, and then Alfie would get out of bed and I'd hear him banging things loudly in the kitchen and I would stare at the concrete wall.

He told me stories of his childhood. Dublin, and then the slums of Birmingham. He tried to describe the smell. Not enough money, unwanted children, a mother who had periods of insanity and who never showed any warmth to him, not once that he could remember.

'I hate her. I *hate* her,' he said. 'I wish she was dead. Surely she'll die soon.' And the Catholic church and the Irish priests looming over it all. His hate for Catholicism seemed to touch on mania and over and over again he would repeat wild stories of priests blessing brothels and taking half the profits. I thought of the sun and the sea and the Anglican Sunday School picnics of the world I had assumed was the only one. Shadows in the late afternoon moving across the lawn behind the cream wooden house with the red roof and my brother and I home from the beach, salt drying on our sunburnt legs, sprawled on the back verandah inventing a code so that we could write secret messages, and reading Captain Marvel comics. Shiny bicycles leaning up against the side of the house and us swinging on the front gate waiting for Dad to appear at the end of the road coming home from his office at the Ministry of Works, we running and running along the hot pavement under the trees to meet him.

Alfie's friend Kenneth often visited us. He had been at the Institution ahead of us, he was divorced and gentle and often on the dole and loved doing crossword puzzles. His pipe smoke would fill the bedroom as we sat on the thin beds, the three of us, drinking coffee and reading a play aloud. *Death of a Salesman* one week. *King Lear* the next. And maybe *The Seagull* on a Sunday evening with a few bottles of beer on the floor beside us. Usually on Sundays we spent an hour first in a draughty pub drinking halves of bitter at a wet-ringed table. Cigarette ash dropped into the beer while people turned their eyes upwards to watch 'Sunday Night at the Palladium'. I'd read plays with them for a while, then I would go to bed and they would talk for hours, mostly Alfie talking and soul-searching and shouting and Kenneth puffing at his pipe and listening and nodding and nodding. One rainy night Kenneth came in, water running down his spectacles, to tell us what had just happened to him in the Gentlemen's Lavatory in Piccadilly Circus Underground.

'There I was quietly peeing when someone called out frantically HOLD IT so I did, we all did, in amazement and with great difficulty I may say and there was a man scrambling about in the thing saying he'd dropped one of his contact lenses, well we all stood, holding it, while he looked but just then the automatic flush went and his contact lens was flushed away and he just sat on the tiles and cried.'

'Let's read *Hamlet* tonight,' said Alfie.

I had never had to worry about money before. I coped very badly with the anxiety about the next electricity bill, the price of meat. We were always turning the heater off when we should have been turning another one on. We had sausages a lot and for lunch every day we had soup and a sandwich at the Institution cafeteria. I remember most of all one cold grey rush-hour evening after a row with Alfie at the Institution walking down the King's Road by myself, knowing there was nothing to eat at the flat counting out my bus fare and finding I didn't have enough to buy a packet of soup. I went back to Islington and wept, lay under the pale green bedspread with my coat and shoes and stockings on it was so cold and cried and cried.

Alfie came home with his script and his voice book and found me lying there in the dark, mascara running, stockings laddered, my wedding ring on the wrong hand.

Chapter V

By the fourth term all the students were tense and shouting and throwing things. The days were dark and grey still and our toothbrushes froze beside the Islington bath and I once tried some hot chestnuts in Oxford Street but they tasted horrible.

In the pub across the road a Danish student of stage-management smiled at me as he played snooker and a Canadian girl cried in a corner. An African from South Africa got slowly drunk at a table and every now and then his laugh, strange and hysterical, would sound above all the other noise. They said, about him, . . . *drugs, he's drugged* . . . but they said so much about so many people. And the rest of us would be sitting there, smoking furiously, talking about the theatre. Scenes we'd done, what we'd felt, what the lecturer had said, what job so-and-so had got soon after leaving the Institution, who had met who at a theatrical party and whether he was a queer or not. I told Alfie I didn't think we had any homosexuals in Australia. He looked at me incredulously and mentioned an Australian we both knew.

I told him I didn't believe him.

He then told me exactly and implicitly what they did, who among our acquaintances did it to whom, and laughed at my shocked face. He then kept singing a Beatles song called 'Penny Lane' and asked me what I thought finger pie was. I said was it a special sausage roll you have in England and he laughed again and told me I was the most naive, bourgeois, middle-class person he'd ever met in his life and that was what was wrong with my acting and then went off to do his voice exercises.

The students got more and more peculiar.

'They're always criticizing me,' Alfie shouted at me. 'I can't act any more I used to be brilliant I know I used to be brilliant but now they've taken away my spontaneity they've made me think about my voice and my ribs and my legs and I can't act any more.' Girls wept even more in the toilets next to the lockers and the old sandshoes and the discarded plastic bags. Men shouted in the pub and smashed beer glasses on the floor. Students got pregnant or married or decided they were queer or had nervous breakdowns. Something was wrong with us but the teachers said we were only going through the Usual Crisis that's all, and nodded their heads in a knowing manner. Alfie blamed me as well as the Institution because he said I had undermined his confidence and made him accept middle-class values. Anthony the architectural student blamed the principal who had never liked him and kept telling him he shouldn't be in the theatre. Julia, in the class above us, blamed the unfairness of the whole world and cried and took pills and said she was going back to Canada where the sun shone. John, who had come straight from school blamed the whole set-up of the Institution which he said was geared to turn us out like standard-English-speaking zombies and took all our natural talent away. Samantha blamed everything on her broken glasses. I decided I'd go home as soon as I'd finished the course. The South African African from the class above just laughed his crazy laugh and got drunk in the pub every night and borrowed money from the barman.

The Institution had attached to it a very well-equipped theatre where for the last part of their course finals students were 'on show' to agents, directors, the critics, the public. This was where we were supposed to end up when we'd passed the Usual Crisis Point.

We waited for the cast lists to go up outside the principal's mahogany-dark study. We smoked more heavily than ever and swooned over an actress from the Moscow Arts Theatre who came to give us a lecture. She was middle-aged and plump and wore a purple dress.

The lists were up.

My first part was Paulina, the old woman in *The Winter's Tale*.

'Someone has to play these parts,' the Principal said to me.

I grimly read through *The Winter's Tale* sitting in the pub waiting for Alfie. I found I was sitting near the South African African. He was talking about South Africa to someone and he wasn't laughing in that funny way like he usually did. I cast a surreptitious glance at the hair, that sort of hair that looked like a pot cleaner. Then suddenly he said 'Oh sh—it man,' and banged on the counter for another drink.

'What will you have man?' he said to the boy he was talking to, and then he saw me sitting next to him.

'What will you have man?' he said to me.

'Oh no thank you,' I said politely, 'no not just now thanks.' He just looked at the cider I was drinking and bought me another one and laughed and all his white teeth gleamed at me.

'So how're you getting on baby, you're from the old Empire just like me do you like the weather?' I thought perhaps he was mocking me but I didn't know how to answer except to discuss the cold and his black face seemed to laugh at me.

'Yeah. Yeah,' he said. 'The winter's bad but what about the summer, down in the Underground man with all those smelling English.'

Spring came and the clocks were put forward and there were daffodils in the parks. When the leaves started shining that golden green on summer evenings again Alfie said to me: 'We must come to terms with the failure of our relationship,' and he packed his cases.

'Yes,' I said, and I put the wedding ring into a box of old brooches and shiny things that I kept to use on the stage. I went back to live with the old lady in Fulham and the net cutrains down the street fluttered to see me back again. Alfie and his friend Kenneth got another basement flat together in Chelsea and one Sunday I went there for a drink but we were all uncomfortable and I didn't go again.

While I was rehearsing *The Winter's Tale* Alfie was in *Romeo and Juliet* which was to go on tour to Scunthorpe and Grimsby so we weren't thrown together too much. But sometimes we passed each other in Institution corridors on the way to rehearsals and we would anxiously and politely enquire how the other was. Our friends who had seen us together for so long weren't quite sure whether to ask us out separately or together. Then Alfie got another girlfriend, a girl with soft long brown hair who was often in the pub across the road and at Institution parties, and he slept with her at a party so everyone knew then and asked us out separately.

Chapter VI

My performance as Paulina, my debut at the Institution was not a marked success. I still couldn't speak perfectly Standard English, so Paulina had a slight Australian accent and there was something not quite right about the wig, it hung greyish and limp around my ears and the director cried despairingly up on to the stage at the dress rehearsal: 'Do you have to look and sound so exactly like a tired Australian surfer?'

I was so petrified on the first night that the stage manager, the Danish boy who I played snooker with in the pub sometimes, had to almost push me on the stage when the lights went up for my entrance.

> *I dare be sworn,* I said,
> *These dangerous unsafe lunes i' the King, beshrew them!*
> *He must be told on't and he shall: the office*

Becomes a woman best; I'll take't upon me.
If I prove honey-mouth'd let me tongue blister,
And never to my red-looked anger be
The trumpet any more.

And above me, quite clearly, I saw the boy in the lighting box so contorted with laughter that he was all bent over in a heap.

When the last cast list of the term went up on the board outside the principal's study and I went to see which old lady I would be playing I found I was to play a young girl after all: Anya in Chekhov's *The Cherry Orchard*. It was rainy August, summer still and I knew that I would soon be free to go home at last. Sometimes I wondered a bit what I would do, but I thought I would think about that later. Just to leave all the greyness. I played snooker in the pub with the Danish stage manager, and drank sometimes with the South African African whose name I learned was Mohale. He had left the Institution but still came back to the pub sometimes and often bought people drinks and told funny stories about the time he had made a film in Morocco, laughing loudly with that strange laugh as he talked. I couldn't help notice how extremely *black* he was, he was the only black person I'd ever actually known and I used to have little surreptitious stares at him when I thought he wasn't looking.

The director of *The Cherry Orchard* was a small angry Greek who shouted at us and made us work very long hours. I was glad. Priscilla, the girl who was playing

Varya, looked very strained sometimes and told me it was because she had had a row with her husband who was an actor and who sometimes stayed out at parties all night.

'I would rather *die*,' she said to me, 'than get pregnant. I will never get pregnant as long as I live. What a life, with screaming kids and your husband going out any time and you stuck there getting ugly and old, God what a fate!'

'Yes,' I said.

We smoked together in a corner of the stuffy rehearsal room whispering about men and love and what part so-and-so had got and who was sleeping with who and whether they were queers or not and the director shouted at the other actors and waved his small arms.

And sometimes I cried a bit again in the Fulham night, from the loneliness. Sundays were the worst, long days full of nothing, and I used to wait for it to be Monday again when I would have something I had to do. One Sunday I said to my landlady that I had a busy day ahead of me, and then I got on a tube with a copy of *The Cherry Orchard* and went all the way to Hampstead Heath. It wasn't very warm but there were lots of people walking, together, carrying big armfuls of Sunday papers. I sat down on a bench for a while but I felt cold. I thought I would go and see Keats' House, but, down an avenue of trees, it was closed. I walked aimlessly down Haverstock Hill wondering whether I should go to the pictures.

'Well, Hi baby.' Mohale's voice and that laugh. He was dressed in a beautiful dark blue suit, and he was with another African in another suit. They crossed the road towards me.

'Come to a party,' said Mohale.

'Oh. Well. I'm sorry I'm busy . . .' I felt foolish because I couldn't have looked very busy kicking at stones down Haverstock Hill. The friend, who had the same pot-cleaner hair smiled at me with white teeth and said, 'Come just for a little while. It's only in Kentish Town.'

I still hesitated, slightly alarmed, but I was so obviously going nowhere and I didn't want them to think I would refuse because they were black, which was the reason really so I smiled a bit and said thank you, I'd come for a little while but couldn't stay for long as I had a lot of work to do and lines to learn and washing to do and . . . I was still talking when they hailed a taxi and told the driver to go to Kentish Town.

That party. It seemed to me that night that I hadn't laughed aloud and sung and danced since I'd been in London. It seemed to me that nearly two grey unlaughing years lay behind me. I laughed all the time. The music was so loud, I could hear it when we got out of the taxi filling the chilly summer late afternoon and I saw the taxi-driver who heard it too purse his lips and look at me in a certain way, harshly. There was a guitar in the corner and when the music stopped somebody would play and everyone would sing strange clicking songs and drink out of bottles. And laugh, laugh at everything, laugh at the music at the singing at me trying to dance at what people said. I was introduced to a few people, there were Africans there, but some white people besides me and some

Indians and some people who were not as black as the others, sort of brown. I'd never seen so many un-white people in my life.

I kept feeling this strange feeling of release, of immense laughter welling up inside me and again and again I kept thinking of lying on the pale green bedspread in the basement flat while Alfie did voice exercises in the next room. I wanted to go to the lavatory and I asked Mohale's friend Jojo where it was. He took my arm and took me down two flights of stairs to a dark lavatory with no toilet paper. He waited for me and I heard him talking to someone in another language and laughing.

'What language was that?' I asked.

'Zulu,' he said to me and took me back upstairs. Zulu I said to myself giggling and we danced again. They danced so *sexily*, the Africans, I kept stopping to watch the loose, moving bodies, I hadn't ever seen anyone dance like that before and that made me laugh more and more. And once I saw Jojo looking at me, sort of puzzled.

And quite clearly I remember I wasn't drunk and I wasn't hysterical I was just dancing in this one room with all these people the music blaring the people laughing bottles everywhere and a sort of smell that only later I was to understand was the smell of Africans.

On Monday the elation was still there. I looked for Mohale but he wasn't anywhere. Jojo had said he would see me again and I wanted to cry out when where, but politely said goodnight at the tube station. He hadn't kissed me and I'd wished he had because I wanted to know what it felt like to be kissed by an African.

On Tuesday *The Cherry Orchard* opened to a smattering of people and I felt sick and my palms sweated as usual and I thought how stupid acting was.

'Very good,' said the small angry director after the performance.

'Thank you,' I said and ran to the pub.

Jojo was there with Mohale and I felt a big jumping in my stomach as I caught sight of him. I wanted to say teach me, teach me to be free like that teach me, teach me to have fun and to laugh, teach me what it feels like to be made love to by an African.

'Hello,' I said politely.

'Hello,' he said and bought me a glass of cider.

The Cherry Orchard was my last play at the Institution and I even had a letter from a theatrical agent saying he had seen my performance and was interested in representing me and would I go and see him.

'Whoopee,' I said quite loudly when the letter arrived in the Institution letter-rack and the naval rating looked over my shoulder and read it and said Jolly Good Show and looked wistful.

The last Saturday, late afternoon after the matinee, I wandered in past the laughing, crying masks to collect my things from my locker. The term was over, the corridors and stairs were empty and quiet, only my own footsteps and the traffic in the distance. Late afternoon sun streamed in the windows, fell across the stairs. There was a smell of floor polish: faint, remembered. Nobody in any of the rooms. That room we did our first mime, that one we had our voice classes, that one Alfie – kissed me – one morning. Dust shines in the rays of sunlight. It is all so – quiet.

I bang my empty locker shut and shout moonooloo maynaylay mawnawlaw meeneelee as I run down the stairs out the door and across the road to the pub.

On the street I meet four of them, four of them who started off the course with me. Samantha is there with new glasses, and David the teacher, and Anthony the architectural student, and John who said the Institution turned us out like sausages. We smile to see each other and go into the pub. We pool our money and buy five half pints of bitter and two packets of crisps. The pub is quiet too, just opened, the same late afternoon sun shining in on to the dark tables that are covered with cigarette burns and marks where glasses have been.

David and Anthony haven't got agents, have started writing, sending photographs to all the repertory companies hoping for jobs, anywhere. Samantha is going to get married to an actor who is so wanted by the National Theatre Company that they have said they will give her a job too. We are all very impressed by this and remember what one of our lecturers once told us.

'In this game' – he called it a game – 'talent is inclined to count about five per cent; the other ninety-five per cent is pure luck, sometimes just being in the right place at the right time.'

'Lucky *lucky* Samantha,' we all say as we sit there, drinking our half pints of bitter, wondering how it will turn out for us all. We indulge in a few nostalgic moments but then start to giggle, remembering it all.

That night after the last performance of *The Cherry Orchard* Anthony the architectural student and I had a race to see who could get out of the building first, ran and ran along the street, shouting, tripping over our belongings, dropping things, and those old stone masks Tragedy and Comedy watched us it seemed: Comedy laughed and Tragedy cried.

Chapter VII

Theatrical Agents are people who are supposed to find actors work and who get ten per cent of their earnings. Actors sit at home waiting for telephone calls from them.

My first week after I left the Institution I went to see the agent who had written to me after seeing *The Cherry Orchard*. I thought a little bit about the sea and the real beaches and the warm Sydney sun but – Jojo had asked me out to dinner on Friday night.

So I shook hands with my new agent (Freddie, call me Freddie, everyone does, and he giggled) and he said I'd be hearing from him soon. Sure enough, two days later a phone call, and I was off to some film studios at Twickenham to audition for a small part in a new Beatles film. I sat in a train in my best pink dress, my hands were sweating and I kept clenching my teeth. A *Beatles film*.

That would give them something to talk about in the old pub and the Institution corridors. I wondered how much they would pay me and what Jojo would say and whether George Harrison would like me. Outside the station I asked the way to the studios in a grocer's shop, wondering why the woman didn't show more interest at hearing my destination. After all, I was going to be in a *Beatles film*. I turned a corner – and there was a band of about a hundred little girls jumping up and down and screaming. At the gate I spoke to a man in a uniform and was allowed through. Ooooooooh cried the little girls pushing in behind me and I heard them crying Aaaaaaah when the gate was locked again. A red light outside a door kept me waiting and there seemed to be a lot of other girls waiting too. I wondered if my Ophelia audition piece would be suitable to do for the director, I'd worked very hard at it. The red light went off and we went into the studio. There were John and Paul and George and Ringo. They were sitting on a set which looked like a room of a house and Ringo wore a purple ring and looked bored. I sort of milled in the crowd of technicians and lights and wires and blondes. There were people everywhere. Then somebody asked me what did I want, I'm auditioning I said, wait a minute he said, for the director. I looked around, somebody had given John a hamburger. Then the director came up to me, looked at me for a second and then said, 'Sorry dear, not sexy enough' and passed on to a girl with long blonde hair and a big bosom. I went out of the studio, past closed doors and along the corridor and out through the gate again. The little girls were waiting.

'*Did you see them did you see them?*' they cried, touching me, pulling at my pink dress.

'*Did you talk to them, do you know them?*' holding on to me, lots of them, not letting me pass, hurting my arm.

'No, no I didn't see them, I didn't,' and I ran up the street to the station hearing them screaming behind me RINGO RINGO RINGO.

I'd told Jojo I'd meet him at Leicester Square. I thought the old landlady and the neighbours behind the net curtains wouldn't approve of an African coming to collect me. He was waiting when I got there and my stomach jumped again when I saw him. He looked beautiful. I suddenly had an immense desire to touch his hair to see if it really was like a pot cleaner but I kept my hands in my pockets and said hello. We'd hardly started walking before he met two friends, Africans, and they were all laughing down Charing Cross Road and I had again that feeling of elation. We all went into a pub for a drink and I noticed lots of people staring, and looking at me the way the taxi-driver had looked at me.

We went to a club that night, Jojo and I, where we danced and ate and drank and I felt so happy I thought something inside me would burst. I told him about the Beatles film and he laughed so much he nearly fell off a chair. I did touch his hair and it felt soft, not like a pot-cleaner at all, and he seemed to understand and he laughed and touched my hair too. And all the time this – free – feeling, old burdens off my shoulders.

At half past two we walked slowly along empty streets

hand in hand. My heels clicked on the pavement.

'I'm going to Dar-es-Salaam tomorrow,' said Jojo.

'Where's Darissalam?' I asked, giggling, feeling his hand dry in mine.

'Africa,' said Jojo.

'Africa,' I said and my stomach gave that jump again. I stopped walking and it was quiet in the street, then a night-bus went past, then it was quiet again.

'Why?' I said.

'Well. Business,' said Jojo.

'But you're a student, aren't you an economics student?' I felt a sudden feeling of panic, I realized I knew nothing about him, he said his name was Jojo and he said he came from South Africa and he said he was just going to start his last year of an economics degree. And he had made me laugh and he had made me happy.

'Yes,' said Jojo, 'I'm an economics student.'

'Did you ask me out and give me a good time and think I'd go home with you and sleep with you and then you could go to Africa?' I said and found I was crying as easily as I'd been laughing just before.

'Don't cry,' said Jojo. He looked . . . puzzled.

'What's your name?' I asked him, feeling the tears running down my cheeks.

'James Mkwayi, I'm always called Jojo,' he said. 'Don't cry.'

I stood on the pavement just crying and thinking do I have to go back to the greyness, I wanted him to teach me, I've just started to learn.

'I expect I'll be back,' he said.

'What about your economics course?'

'Well, I hope to come back to it soon,' he said. 'It depends. On the business.'

'I want a taxi,' I said. I stood sniffing and blowing my nose on a tissue and not saying anything while we waited for a taxi in the quiet streets. When it came Jojo put his arms round me and kissed me. It didn't feel like an African kissing me, it felt like someone going away.

Chapter VIII

The autumn came, leaves everywhere, and I watched the evenings getting darker and felt the coldness in the air and looked up Dar-es-Salaam on a map and cried sometimes in my upstairs Fulham room.

'I'm stupid,' I told myself. 'I'm always crying about something.'

After I'd spent weeks auditioning for jobs I didn't get, and counting the number of other actresses auditioning, and waiting for the phone to ring, my agent phoned to say Great News Darling, and told me that I was to start work in a week for a repertory company up north that I'd auditioned for, nine pounds a week for rehearsals, fourteen pounds a week for playing. It sounded like a lot of money, and work at last. I wanted to celebrate but who with, still I went out and sat in a pub and bought myself a double brandy which cost seven and twopence.

'Cheers,' I said to myself, 'cheers', and thought wistfully of all that laughter. The streets seemed full of black people. I'd heard people say all blacks look alike, but I scanned the faces and nobody looked like Jojo.

I packed some bags, left strict instructions with the old lady in Fulham about any messages, got on a train, and travelled north on an autumn English day pouring with rain so that the brown and yellow leaves lay all soggy on the roads and beside the railway tracks. I felt very nervous: my first job, there I was, a professional actress on the northbound train having a Guinness and a sandwich, a professional actress, an actress. But Jojo in Dar-es-Salaam.

At first rehearsals of a new company everyone looks at everyone else, pretending not to, wondering about each other, sizing each other up. By the end of the day the rehearsal room smells of stale cigarette smoke, and dirty cups rest on window sills, and I have nowhere to stay the night.

'You could spend the night at Suzy's,' someone suggests. Suzy is a seventeen-year-old Assistant Stage Manager and earns five pounds a week.

'Yes, come and stay with me,' she says, 'if you don't mind cats.' So we go on a bus with one of my suitcases to Suzy's room. It is on the top floor. As she unlocks her door a little kitten flies out and jumps up into her arms. It has made two puddles beside her bed. Another large cat is asleep on a chair. Suzy loves them and cuddles them. It is a large room, smelling strongly of cats and just now the sun has come bleakly out and shines in through the big window and across the wooden floor. She makes soup in the communal kitchen she shares with two actors in the company and we listen to her transistor radio and she tells me a bit about the people in the company. She wants to be an actress and has lots of photos of herself above her bed. She tells me about all her boyfriends and the cats jump around and rub against us and mew. She pulls out a couch and gives me two blankets: 'It has a broken spring but you can sort of twist yourself round it,' she says. Then she goes back to the theatre for the evening performance and I'm left with the cats. I stare out of the window at the red and yellow evening trees. Dar-es-Salaam I say to myself.

After a long time just sitting, I pick up my copy of *Picnic* and work on my lines until Suzy comes back. We have cocoa and toast and then go to bed and she tells me more about all her boyfriends and then switches off the light. I curl around the broken spring. I am just falling asleep when something jumps on my neck. The kitten. I put it on the floor, it jumps up immediately. I put it on the floor four times, finally I give up. The kitten spends the night in my hair settling just above my ear, and I spend the night – my first night as a professional actress – curling round a broken spring with a kitten on my head while lines from *Picnic* drift through my mind and I hear a lavatory chain being pulled sometimes on the floor below.

It wasn't a very good company. At rehearsals people didn't seem to care much, especially the director, who often just read the stage directions out of the script and told us that would do. *Picnic* was just another play: there had been one two weeks ago, there was one on now, and as soon as *Picnic* opened rehearsals would begin for the next one. After the keenness everyone at the Institution had had about their work I was taken by surprise. Yet in the teashop over the cinema where most of the company gathered the talk was exactly the same: what job so-and-so had got, who had met who at a party, whether a well-known actor was a queer or not, and who was sleeping with who. I found a drivers' cafe with a juke-box and sneaked away there sometimes and had egg and chips and kept playing a record called 'I Hear the Sound of Distant Drums' and the drivers laughed.

And every Friday lunch-time I received a plain brown envelope with my pay inside.

I got a room with a family who thought the theatre was romantic and asked me if I knew Peter O'Toole. Every morning I walked from their house to the theatre through an autumn park, it was cold and there were leaves blowing and falling along the paths and over the grass. I liked the sound of the leaves as I walked through them. Yet I felt only half alive. I wondered if I'd been only half alive all my life till that Sunday afternoon when I got out of the taxi and the music was so loud. I thought about when I was young and the sun was shining and my brother and I and days in sticky summer offices with the sound of typewriters and parties on beaches and skiing holidays in winter and the first days I knew Alfie when

45

I felt so sophisticated. I couldn't have spent all that time being only half alive, I must have been happy. And yet that bursting feeling, that sort of tension, the – awareness – of those few times with Jojo and that warmth and – laughing. The yellow leaves blew drily across the grass past the empty wooden grandstand painted green and on to the lake where the ducks swam.

Plays at the theatre opened every second Tuesday. On the Monday night the dress-rehearsal of *Picnic* went on until 4 a.m. because there was so much trouble with the lights. The director screamed and shouted at everybody and I tore my dress on the iron railing outside the dressing-room door. I felt nervous and depressed and the theatre was cold and draughty and I wondered why anyone should think being an actress was glamorous. I couldn't get any taxis at 4 o'clock in the morning so I started to walk back to my room. A police car stopped me.

'Rather late for you to be walking around, miss.'

'Oh,' I said.

'Where have you been? It's a quarter past four in the morning.'

'I've been working at the theatre.'

'Oh,' said the policeman and shone a torch at me. 'Well. Sorry. We thought you might be someone else, there's been a complaint laid about a girl in a brown raincoat being raped in an empty house.'

I started to giggle. 'I'm tired,' I said.

'We'll take you home,' said the policeman. So they delivered me to my door and I went to bed and dreamt of Jojo laughing and dancing with policemen in a small place lit with coloured lights called Dar-es-Salaam.

Next evening I saw my face quite white in the mirror. The harsh globes round the glass hurt my eyes and my palms were wet. I had received a couple of good luck cards from people and a telegram from my agent wishing me 'Great good luck in your debut as a professional actress'. The director came in to wish us luck.

'Lovely performance you're giving darling, truly lovely,' he said to me.

'Darling,' he said to Estelle, kissing her, 'you're as wonderful as ever.'

'Marvellous, darling,' he said to Jenny. The other actresses in the dressing room were complaining about their costumes and the coldness of the theatre, they didn't seem nervous at all.

'Five minutes please,' said the Stage Manager.

My make-up didn't seem to help me look much better and my legs felt stiff. I tried to remind myself that it was just the same as acting in the theatre at the Institution. Then that reminded me of the lighting technician laughing at me and falling over in the lighting box.

I didn't enjoy it at all. I felt that the production wasn't very good, and that I wasn't very confident and I remember wondering if this was all my training meant. The local paper the next day said that I gave a 'very nice performance'.

I worked in that company for nearly three months and got quite used to being an actress and working long hours in a cold theatre and not being satisfied with the results. The other two actresses who were in the company all the time I was there kept complaining that all men were queers. One of them, Estelle, had been in the same company for four years. She looked at each new man who arrived hungrily, hopelessly. She had been in the theatre for sixteen years and was still waiting for the break, the luck, the chance, the Big Time.

One of the leading actors who'd sat with a patronizing arm around me at a party at Suzy's place, pushed me up against a wall outside the Stage Manager's office one afternoon after rehearsal. He kissed me with his tongue inside my mouth and then whispered into my ear: 'I fancy you.' He was just putting his hand up under my jersey when the Stage Manager's phone rang.

'See you later, darling,' and he ran down the stairs.

I stood there against the wall where he left me while the phone rang on and on and nobody answered. I wondered if Jojo would ever come back from Dar-es-Salaam and if I'd ever feel his arms around me again or whether the grey life would simply continue as before and people would put their hands under my jersey. I wondered again what the business could be in Dar-es-Salaam, why hadn't I asked him more, why hadn't I asked if I could write to him, why hadn't I gone home with him that night instead of crying and getting into a taxi. I thought for the hundredth time that if he'd gone all the way to Africa and back on business he wouldn't be very likely to still have my phone number on a piece of paper in his pocket. The phone in the Stage Manager's office stopped ringing and the grey cold theatre was quiet. Down below on the street the town's grey rush-hour traffic was moving slowly in the grey evening. Despair welled up inside me and I ached and ached.

Darling, I cried, *Anyone, Darling*. It seemed to be aloud, but perhaps it was to myself. No answer anywhere. Everyone was out having tea before the evening show.

After my last performance there I caught an empty Sunday morning train back to London.

At the first stop a middle-aged man got on carrying a brief-case like my father used to have. He sat opposite me. He was balding a bit, looked quite ordinary and I read the *Sunday Times*.

'Do you mind,' he said, looking partly at me and partly at the houses flashing past us, 'if I drink?' No one else was sitting near.

'No,' I said, hoping he wasn't going to be difficult, 'no, of course not.'

From his brief-case he brought a bottle of whisky and a small empty clean Marmite jar. He poured the whisky very carefully into the jar. I buried my head in the *Sunday Times* wondering why he found whisky necessary at 7.45 a.m.

The houses passed, and some fields, and the smell of whisky was strong mixed in with the smell of the train. I wondered when I'd get another job. And I wondered about Dar-es-Salaam.

'Excuse me.' He was holding the whisky bottle and the Marmite jar towards me. 'Perhaps you would like . . .?'

The pale yellow liquid moved quite beautifully inside the bottle with the movement of the train.

'Thank you,' I said and he poured me half a Marmite jar full.

By the time the train pulled in at Euston Station the whisky bottle was almost empty and we were both drunk. Neither of us had said a word to the other except 'Will you have another,' and 'Thank you, after you,' and there was a mutual looking out of the window with no bottle in sight as the guard took our tickets and noticed that the smell of alcohol was very strong.

When the train stopped the man put the almost empty bottle and the Marmite jar into his brief-case and stood up slowly and carefully.

'I would like' – he paused, leaning on the back of the seat, 'to wisshsh you well.'

'I would like,' I said, still sitting, 'to wish you well too.' He didn't smile, bowed rather, and lumbered out of the carriage. I sat there for a while until a woman came through to clean the carriage. She was black and brusque and told me to hurry up she had a lot of work to do. I wanted to ask her if she knew Jojo but she glared at me with such venom and wrinkled her nose in distaste at the smell of the whisky or perhaps the smell of me, so I picked up my two cases and stumbled onto the platform. I had two cups of black coffee next to the ladies waiting room on the station and felt terrible. It was eleven o'clock in the morning. When I finally staggered back to the house in Fulham the old lady was at church and the other two boarders were playing cards by a smokeless-fuel fire in the sitting-room with the green vases and the television set and Bless This House on the wall. There were several letters for me and a message from 'Spotlight' and a Christmas parcel from an aunt in Australia containing three lace handkerchiefs wrapped round a picture of the Sydney Harbour Bridge.

Chapter IX

My agent said there were lots of hopeful things happening and I wasn't to get depressed.

I decided I would get a room to live in on my own, not in Fulham, not with old ladies, not with boarders. I walked up and down streets that cold December looking on notice-boards, calling in at agencies. One afternoon, drinking a cup of coffee in a cafe in Camden Town and seeing my nose red in the mirror, I suddenly also saw Mohale in the mirror. I jumped off the stool and turned round, and it was Mohale, with an African girl.

'Mohale,' I said, 'Mohale.'

'Hello baby, how are you?'

'Mohale Mohale is Jojo back from Dar-es-Salaam?'

He looked at me and the girl looked at me and it seemed to me they passed a quick look between them.

Then the girl just continued drinking coffee and looking out of the steamy window on to the street.

'No baby, he's not back yet. I hear there's a spot of trouble but he'll be back one of these fine days.'

'Have you heard from him then?'

'No, no I haven't heard from him. I heard from my friends in the A.N.C.'

'What's the A.N.C.?'

Mohale laughed, that laugh that used to sometimes echo round the Institution.

'Well baby, the A.N.C. that's the African National Congress.'

'What's the African National Congress?'

The girl looked round at me sharply as though I'd said something wrong and I felt myself blushing.

'I just' – I seemed to stutter – 'Well, I just wondered where he was.'

Mohale laughed again, that strange slow laugh.

'He'll come back baby, don't you fret baby, he'll come back.' He said it soothingly, like a song, as if he was singing a song, don't you fret baby, he'll come back baby. . . . And he smiled at me and I got the feeling that there was nothing else to say so I smiled a bit at him too, while the girl looked out of the window again.

'Goodbye,' I said.

'Goodbye baby. Take care of yourself.'

And I went out into the street again, winter in Camden Town.

That very afternoon I found my room. In Camden Town. *£5 per week lovely room share bathroom and toilet* *own kitchen.* The accommodation agent took me himself.

'It really is very nice dear,' he said, 'and no landlady on the premises.' He twinkled his eyes, 'An actress are you,' he ran his tongue over his lips, 'well, we know what actresses are,' and he unlocked the front door of a dirty looking block over a shop. Up two flights of stairs was my room, and somehow, it was nice. No green bed-spreads. It was small but with a big window looking out on to a side street and a large divan bed and a table and a wardrobe and somebody had left orange curtains and the room looked – welcoming – on that winter day with Mohale's sing-song voice in my mind, don't fret baby, don't fret baby.

'Shillings in that meter there for the gas heater,' said the man, 'sixpence in this meter here in the kitchen for the gas stove. No hot water up here but a lovely bath-room downstairs it really is a lovely bathroom.' The kitchen was more like a box than a room, a small stove with two rings on it, a sink with one tap over it, a couple of shelves. A small window looked out on to the concrete walls of other houses, sudden visions of my mother's all-electric kitchen looking at the sea. I went downstairs with the agent to the lovely bathroom. The bath had an old gas water heater at one end, and there was a new basin with toothbrushes on the edge of it. A pipe ran from the water heater to the basin so you could have hot water in the basin as well as in the bath. A door at the back went through to the lavatory.

'Pennies in here for hot water for the bath,' said the man. 'Public phone there outside the bathroom door.'

'Who else lives here?' I asked him.

'Oh, only four others,' he said. 'Two small rooms down here next to the bathroom, a lady in one a gentleman in the other, and a married couple in the room next to yours with their own kitchen. The haberdashery woman in the shop below lives in Hendon. Two weeks' rent in advance.'

'All right,' I said.

'Make *sure*,' I said loudly to the old lady at Fulham, 'that you give this phone number to anybody who rings. I might miss . . . work and . . . things.'

On the tube in the rush-hour one day I met Anna, the professional actress from California who was in my class at the Institution. She was very theatrical, she called people Darling in a loud voice – just the way actresses are supposed to. We had had terrible times in those voice classes, trying to lose our accents and speak Standard English the way they wanted.

'Darling,' she cried to me in a loud voice across the squashed together people and the *Evening Standard*s. 'Darling so *much* has happened. They tried to send me back to America, the bloody Home Office wouldn't extend my permit – as if I actually *like* their lousy English weather.' An *Evening Standard* rattled, bristled a little beside us, or perhaps it was just the movement of the train.

'To get a job, darling, *any* job, well, you know I haven't even got an agent, I wrote to simply every TV director and every repertory company in the whole country, I was desperate, I really was desperate, anyway you know I used to live with Johnnie Peters, well I just had to swallow my pride and go back to him and he got me a year's contract in his company and the Home Office let me stay.' She lit a cigarette in the crowded carriage, pushing a bit to get nearer to me.

'Have you seen Alfie?' she asked, casually.

'No.'

She smiled. 'Oh well darling, that's life, that's life.'

'Have you seen any of the others?' I asked her.

'Well. Jennifer-Anne.'

'Well?'

'Oh darling, we don't speak now, not since that Institution tour of *Romeo and Juliet* to Scunthorpe and Grimsby, really it was unbelievable, we had to share a bedroom and she kept bringing Jonson Taylor in night after night and I kept having to go and sleep with . . .' she looked at me and flicked her cigarette ash, casually, '. . . someone else. Really it was too much having to get up and play Juliet every day after that!'

The *Evening Standard*s became positively rigid and heads looked out from behind and regarded us. *Actresses.*

My agent rings up and asks would I like to take a tiny part in a television play, a two-lined secretary. Thirty-five pounds. Money for Christmas, he says.

'All right,' I answer.

I spend two days rehearsing in a Church Hall. I say: *Mr Braithwaite called Sir* and *Is that all Sir*. The others have been rehearsing for more than two weeks and are rather patronizing towards me.

'Do watch that Australian accent,' are the only words the director says to me.

We spend two days in the television studios. There are lights and ropes and people wearing earphones and cameras. On the second evening the programme is taped. It seems to be a mystery with a murder in it. I feel very nervous as I say *Mr Braithwaite called, Sir* and I hope I am standing in the right place.

Afterwards everyone says to each other Darling wasn't it ghastly and What about when I . . . and Oh Darling didn't I look terrible on the monitor. Someone includes me in the general invitation to have a drink upstairs in the Club. But when I get there nobody notices me or speaks to me. I buy a glass of cider and hold it nervously. Everyone is talking and laughing. But it is not the kind of laughter I dream of. I finish my drink and put the glass down and go home to my room in Camden Town with the orange curtains.

Christmas week and I walk under the Regent Street decorations and buy presents for the old lady in Fulham and the children of the Australian family who have asked me and lots of other Australians to spend Christmas Day with them. It feels as though it is going to snow, that heavy low grey-brown feeling in the sky. Rich with my TV earnings I go into a pub in Leicester Square, that one with all the windows and buy a double brandy for myself and watch all the Christmas people.

'Well, well.'

I looked up and saw a boy who had been ahead of me at the Institution. Winston. He bought himself a drink and sat down next to me and told me about a television play he had just been doing and about the affair he'd been having with the leading actress who was sex-starved. I listened to him and looked out at the people passing and thought of Jojo. And suddenly I saw Alfie walking towards me. I'd thought he was in Manchester, working. I instinctively moved back, away from the window. He was striding along in his aggressive way, deep in thought, wearing that old brown jacket. I had worn that jacket so often – in the rain, in the cold, in the middle of the night getting up to go to the lavatory across that concrete path – it had holes in the lining of the pockets.

Alfie walked past, not seeing me, carrying some books.

And I drank some brandy rather quickly and supposed to myself as Winston talked that the world is full of people like Alfie and me, people who have been unsuccessfully together, shared such intimate, personal times; people who know such – things – about each other. Who later only pass each other in the street. My fingers were around my brandy glass yet they could feel the torn brown lining hidden in Alfie's pocket as he walked away across the street, dodging the traffic disappearing.

'Goodbye,' I say to Winston and go out into the crowds. I walk through part of Soho to Carnaby Street. Everyone sort of consciously swings, Christmas in Swinging London. I try to be one of the Swingers too. Pop music blares out from all the shops into the street. I push into one of the shops to try on a very very short mini-dress. In the tiny changing rooms there are sexy pictures of men, partly in and partly out of bathing shorts, all hairy.

I don't buy the dress, it looks a bit funny with my legs. Someone once told me I had lucky legs and I smiled, feeling pleased, but he said I mean lucky they don't snap when you stand on them. Out into the crowded pushing blaring street again, past all the men's clothes shops: purple shirts green trousers lemon socks. More pictures of men. More pop music. Tourists taking pictures of themselves leaning by the sign that says Carnaby Street.

Back at Piccadilly Circus I feel very depressed. The greyness has all come back again, pale green bedspreads and concrete walls and chilly Sunday evening pubs where glasses stand on old tables and people watch the telly and there is no such person as Jojo. It is only one o'clock and I have nothing to do all day except sign on the dole. So I go into another pub and order myself another double brandy and comfort myself thinking that women used to be extravagant about hats when they were depressed, and I don't wear them.

Government seats in the Berwick Street Soho Employment Exchange (Actresses Section). I sit down to wait my turn and listen to the high chattering women's voices. It is warm and there are travel posters of sunshine and sea on the walls and there is a smell of damp clothes and a mixture of perfumes, and umbrellas make puddles in the corners.

Jennifer-Anne, the starlet from my class at the Institution, comes in in a fur coat and hat.

'Hello Jennifer-Anne.'

'Hello how are you?'

'I'm fine. I thought you were working on a film.'

'Oh. Yes. I've finished that. It was with Cary Grant only they cut out all my scenes. But I'm going to do another one, they're doing a new horror film in February.' She waves and smiles to someone across the room. 'Hey,' she says to me, 'did you hear about Samantha? She's left the National Theatre, she kept missing her entrances and in one of the plays she tripped on her costume and fell over. And her husband kept hitting her, not for tripping over I mean, but because he was jealous or something, anyway she's doing TV commercials now and making lots of money.' We laugh.

'Have you seen Alfie?' she says.

'No,' I answer, but she has seen someone else she knows and is gone, joins a long queue of unemployed actresses on the other side of the room, talking, laughing, patting someone's poodle.

The voices chatter like birds.

'Darling, I *just missed* this fantastic TV lead . . .'

'. . . Did you hear about Suzy? Still it's a *terrible* play. Is she still living with David – mind you I have it on very good authority that he's gay anyway.'

'. . . Caroline is using the coil . . .'

'. . . and so I *nearly* got the part, of course if I'd known the director as well as *she* did . . .'

'Where are you living now?'

'. . . and I start an 'Avengers' episode in ten days' time . . .'

'. . . I was dancing in Holland . . .'

'Next please.' And I sign on the dotted line. 'We're closing this branch,' said the woman with grey hair behind the counter. 'Sign on next time at the Chadwick Street Branch in Westminster. Next please.'

I shiver a bit as I walk out into Soho. It is freezing. The strip clubs in the alleys are open, a man stands guarding the door of one of them eating a hamburger and slow midnight music – a crying, mourning clarinet – wafts out into the narrow alleys in the early afternoon, the sound caught and lost again in the icy biting wind.

They are cold, those ones selling fruit and toothpaste off their barrows and me too I'm cold and I haven't got a job and it's sleeting and Jojo is in Dar-es-Salaam and one of my shoes leaks and I'm an actress.

Chapter X

Towards the end of February I feel as though I have been always sitting there, looking out of my window into the side street, watching the snow, listening for the telephone. I know I should take a typing job. I begin to worry about each shilling I put into the meter, and I read the 'Situations Vacant' columns in the *Evening Standard* and hear again the clicking of typewriters in my mind.

Then one morning my agent rang me, very excited.

'Look your best,' he said. 'Go to the Savoy Hotel at 3.40, ask for Joseph Rubens?'

'Joseph Rubens? The movie producer?'

'Yes yes yes, he's doing a *very big* movie, wants an actress to play an Australian secretary, so of course darling I suggested you, now darling, it's terribly exciting, I want you to go in there and make up to him, flatter him, smile at him, it's a wonderful opportunity, mind you it's only two or three lines, but quite a few scenes where you don't speak, could be three or four days' filming, you know, and it's *contacts*, contacts, meeting people, getting to know people, being with the right people, has marvellous stars and *Sean Connery*, now darling as soon as you get back from the Savoy ring me and let me know how you got on, you must look as neat as possible and for once you won't have to try to hide the Australian accent ho ho ring me dear, bye!'

So I had a bath, washed my hair, ironed my pink dress, cut my nails, dressed carefully, did my hair neatly, practised a few good Australian phrases. I tried not to be excited, I had been excited for too many interviews.

It was freezing cold and the Camden Town tube station was all slushy with old snow and rain. I wore gum boots, carrying my high-heeled shoes in a bag and I wore an old navy-blue cardigan over my pink dress under my coat.

The Savoy Hotel. Greyish cream and greyish purple ornateness. I got directed to the appropriate place by a uniformed little boy. I went up in lifts, along carpeted corridors, past rooms called Patience and Iolanthe. I looked for a Ladies to change my shoes and take off my cardigan. An attendant looked at me suspiciously while I brushed my hair. Then I walked along more carpeted corridors, I kept coming out into empty lounges or seeing myself with newly washed hair in large gilt mirrors. Finally I was ushered into a little ante-room where five other girls were sitting. From long experience of interviews I had brought a book which I could at least pretend to read while covertly keeping an eye on proceedings.

Girls were sent into the inner rooms, came out quickly, went away, more girls arrived. At about a quarter to five a man asked me who I was. I gave my name. He said very nicely sorry to have kept you waiting, come with me and I was ushered into a room with yellow light shades. A fat man looked at me.

'Oh God no not for the bathroom attendant, she's not sexy enough.'

'No no for the Australian secretary.'

'Oh. Have you made any films?'

'Oh, yes, I've played small parts in lots of films.' (This was a useful lie taught me by other actresses in other interview rooms who said never admit you've done *no* filming, say small parts in films.)

'Is that an Australian accent?'

'Yes.'

Two phones started ringing almost simultaneously, and I was forgotten entirely. I stood waiting, on one leg and then the other. Talk about dollars and schedules crackled on the telephones. The fat man looked up at me, stared at me, waved me away. I went out along the carpeted corridors, past the gilt mirrors, out on to the Strand. At the nearest pub I had a Guinness, changed my shoes, put on my cardigan and talked to myself about the stupidity of actresses feeling humiliated.

I saw something in the paper that night about the African National Congress having an argument with the Pan-African Congress, it didn't mention Jojo or Dar-es-Salaam but I cut out the piece and read it over and over again.

Two days later my agent rang me.

'Well my darling, very sly of you not to phone me, *what* an impression you made on Rubens, only too *delighted* to have you on the picture, not much money of course, still twenty-five pounds per day for a guaranteed three days, that's not to be sneered at, starting in about ten days, the Wardrobe Mistress will ring next week to arrange about clothes and darling you are *Sean Connery's* secretary, lucky you dear wish it was me, be nice to him, try to make him notice you, like you, you've got to make the most of these contacts, bye.'

That night I had been invited to dinner by the girl I went to school with in Australia who had married an English school-teacher and lived in Tooting Bec. The ones whose floor I'd slept on when I first arrived. On the crowded steamy tube there were so many black faces and I looked, as I always did, for Jojo. Umbrellas and boots and coats and people looking so cold, and the toes of one of my feet gone numb.

As I sat by a kerosene heater eating stew in their flat in Tooting Bec I told my friend about my job and I heard myself making it sound a bit bigger and a bit more important than it really was and saying 'Sean Connery you know the James Bond man' several times. My friend, Louise, loved it, she kept saying well now I know a film star, isn't it marvellous, now you'll have lots of money, I suppose soon you won't talk to *us*.

'Don't be silly,' I said.

'Well. A real film star,' she said over and over again.

I went on the last tube back to my room in Camden Town, climbed the creaky stairs, put on the heater to try to warm the room, put the kettle on for a cup of tea and a hot water bottle, read the paragraph about the African National Congress, and went to bed. Next door the married couple were having a fight and shouting at one another. After a while it was quiet, and I lay for a long time cuddling my hot water bottle, sometimes hearing cars and once someone coming up the stairs to the floor below. I wondered if I really would be a film star and where Jojo was and about the summer in Australia and the hot hot sun where I never wore cardigans.

On Saturday morning the phone rang.

'Hello,' I said.

'Hello,' said Jojo.

The leaping feeling in my stomach and the numbers people had scrawled on the wall by the telephone with pencils and ball-point pens and someone running a bath in the bathroom just by the telephone.

'Are you back from Dar-es-Salaam?' I said.

'Yes,' he said.

Someone had written EVERTON in big letters on the wall by the telephone.

'Hello,' I said. 'Jojo, Jojo?'

'Shall we meet,' he said, 'shall we meet at that corner at Leicester Square at nine o'clock.'

'Yes goodbye,' I said.

All day I felt nervous and tense and happy and sad and excited. I washed my hair. I kept reminding myself not to get excited about auditions then remembering it wasn't an audition. I cried, then stopped crying thinking it would make me look awful. I mustn't expect too much,

I mustn't expect anything, I don't know anything about him what is the African National Congress he's probably been back for months O God let me not expect too much and then be disappointed.

He was reading a newspaper. He looked, again – beautiful. He was wearing dark green trousers and a lighter green shirt and a short grey overcoat. His hair looked like a pot cleaner again. There were lots of people passing and sometimes they bumped into him and he just moved a little bit and kept on reading. His fingers were long and brown holding the newspaper. I was almost too scared to interrupt him, my knees felt funny. I waited for two or three minutes, looking at him, and he didn't look up once, he just kept reading and reading in the lights from the street and the buildings.

'Jojo,' I said finally.

He looked up surprised, then his face sort of cleared as he saw me and his white teeth shone.

'Hello baby,' he said. 'Let's go and have a drink.'

I watched him as he walked towards the table with the drinks.

'Jojo,' I said, before he'd even settled down in his chair, 'Jojo,' I was afraid he'd disappear again before I'd found out more about him, 'Jojo, what's the African National Congress?'

He just looked at me for a while, then he smiled and moved his shoulders getting more comfortable and said: 'The African National Congress is the main African political party of South Africa. It is banned from South Africa and has its headquarters in Dar-es-Salaam. I'm attached to the offices in London as well as being an economics student. Now have you been making any more Beatles films?' And he picked up his glass and laughed at me. I told him about being a film star the week after next and working in repertory and the cats. Some Africans came past and said, Hello man, and Good to see you man, and talked for a moment and looked interestedly at me and then went away again.

'Let's go to a club,' said Jojo later so we went dancing and laughing and drinking till two o'clock in the morning. I kept thinking this is what it means being happy, this loud music and this dancing and me and Jojo talking, and he sat with his arm around me and laughed at me again when I touched his hair to remember what it felt like.

When we came out on to the street it was raining and the wind was like a knife cutting through my coat and past my pink dress to my insides. Jojo put his arm around me, his coat flapping in the wind. He was looking for a taxi.

'Jojo,' I said.

He looked at me and I put my hand up to his wet crinkly hair. He kissed me and I could feel the rain on our faces and it wasn't like those movies of two people kissing in the rain very sexy, it was freezing cold the rain was coming inside my shoes and I could see in the street lights his black face with rain running down it. The wind whipped the rain along the street slantingly under the lights and I could feel it through my coat through my pink dress.

'Jojo, you won't put me in a taxi and send me home again?'

'Are you crying again?' he said.

'No,' I answered, 'no it's the rain you look as though you're crying too I'm not crying,' I said laughing, 'I'm not,' but I was. Tears and rain all mixed up on my cold face, wanting so much to stay with him.

'I wasn't thinking of sending you home baby.' And he smiled under the street lights and wet and cold I smiled too, smiling as the icy wind blew the rain against me in his arms.

Jojo lived in a house in Kentish Town. The house was owned by the African National Congress. There were seven rooms in the house and a big communal living room and a bathroom and a kitchen. Africans lived in all the rooms, African students or perhaps they weren't students Jojo just said They're all students, when I asked him. That first cold raining night when I went there with Jojo in a taxi there was a party in one of the rooms, people singing and a gramophone blaring, lovely. We were soaking wet. Jojo pushed me into the bathroom with a red towel and a white dressing gown. The bathroom was old. There was a rust stain in the bath and the hot water geyser was old like the one at my place. I looked for a meter to put pennies in but there didn't seem to be one, I took off my wet clothes and put on the dressing gown and rubbed my hair with the towel. I didn't know whether to leave all my clothes on the bath to dry or not, I was just thinking about this, rubbing my hair, when the door opened and an African girl came in, dressed in a long yellow and black winding around dress.

'Oh,' she said, seeing me.

'Oh I'm just going, I got caught in the rain,' I said, gathering all my wet clothes, feeling embarrassed.

'I see,' said the African girl and waited for me to go, hostile.

I went back up the stairs to Jojo's room but he wasn't there and for just a second I thought panicking that he'd gone away and left me again, but then I heard him talking on the stairs and laughing. There was a heater on and I put my clothes near it to dry. There were lots and lots of books in the room and a table and a wardrobe and a bed with a cover made with brightly designed material. A big cheap looking alarm clock on the floor by the bed, ticking loudly. That was all really, quite an empty *impersonal* room. But lots and lots of books. I sat on the bed and waited. I couldn't hear Jojo talking any more. I could hear the singing from below but not very loudly. The clock ticked and the heater hummed. I felt warm and I shivered and I waited for Jojo.

Next morning I opened my eyes and saw a brown arm resting on my white arm and remembered that I was in a flat in Kentish Town full of Africans. Jojo was still asleep. I put my hand on his hair which no longer felt strange to me and looked at the smooth smooth dark brown skin of his face. I could hear people moving about in the house and a record playing. The curtains moved a bit and I could hear the wind and rain outside. I felt again the same bursting happiness in my stomach, a physical feeling.

The door opened suddenly and an African came half into the room. I felt myself blushing.

'Oh sorry man,' he said to me, smiling, not embarrassed at all and he closed the door and went out again. Jojo slept on. I moved a bit and looked down at the alarm clock on the floor by the bed. Twenty past ten. Sunday morning. The rain outside. Jojo's arm and part of his chest not covered by the blankets were dark brown and I looked very white next to him. The air in the room was cold. I snuggled down closer to him and in his sleep his arm tightened around me. I lay there feeling happy and secure and fell asleep.

A knock on the door, 'Jojo telephone.' Jojo groaned.

'All right,' he called out. 'Hello,' he said to me, kissing me.

'I love you,' I said.

'Jojo come on man, it's Dr Mkady, he's just arrived from Tunisia.'

'I'm coming,' called Jojo. He smiled at me and kissed me again and got out of bed. His body was brown and smooth and he put on the white dressing gown and he looked to me like a Prince of somewhere.

'I have to go to a meeting,' said Jojo, coming back with two red tin mugs of coffee. He sat on the edge of the bed brown in his white dressing gown, drinking the coffee from the red mug. Another black head appeared round the door.

'Oh come in,' said Jojo, 'it's all right,' and a thin African came in, not the one who'd come in earlier in the morning.

'This is Henry,' said Jojo, introducing us, and I felt myself blushing and I bent my head over the coffee so that my hair might hide my face.

Jojo and Henry started talking about the meeting.

'We don't want any trouble with the Pac boys,' said Henry, 'the Press will be there now that Mkady's arrived and . . .'

'No man, I don't think there'll be that kind of trouble,' interrupted Jojo. 'I saw Roberta yesterday she said that Jonas had been into the Anti-Apartheid office and they . . .'

The words rumbled on meaning nothing to me. I drank my coffee, lay back in bed, watched Jojo, looked at the room. I wanted to go to the lavatory. I didn't have any clothes on. Jojo and Henry talked on and on. I wondered whether they'd even notice if I got up out of bed naked. I got more and more uncomfortable and the room was cold. Once I saw Henry looking at me while he was talking, he smiled when I caught his eye and looked away, still talking. I didn't like his smile as much as Jojo's. And he had a funny eye, damaged, stitched around, not quite straight.

'Jojo,' I said finally, urgently, 'I *must* go to the lavatory.'

They both laughed and Henry said 'Oh sorry,' and he went out and Jojo laughed at me again as I got out of bed shy, cold, white, naked, he pulled me inside his dressing gown for a minute rubbing my back making me warm again. I wanted to say I love you.

'Can I come to the meeting?' I asked him.

He looked surprised. He took off the dressing gown and gave it to me and put on some trousers.

'Yes, if you want to. It's a political meeting about South Africa.'

'Oh,' I said. 'Oh. Good.'

I opened the door of the room and went downstairs to the bathroom. A record was playing loudly from somewhere, sadly.

> *... I'm watching the sea*
> *Will the one I love*
> *Be coming back*
> *To me——ee. ...*

The bathroom door was open, inside *another* African was shaving.

'Oh God, excuse me,' I said, 'could I just go to the lavatory?'

'Sure,' said the African, he looked funny, white foam on his black face, he just leant on the wall outside waiting.

'Thank you,' I said, coming out again. He moved himself off the wall, lazily like a cat, and sauntered back into the bathroom.

I went slowly back up the stairs, my feet cold and white on the bare boards, the music following me, achingly.

> *I cover the waterfront*
> *I'm watching the sea*
> *Will the one I love*
> *Be coming back*
> *To me.*

The meeting was held in a small hall in Westminster.

It was about half full, people scattered all round the hall, white, black, some Indians, I thought I saw the African who had put his head round the door of Jojo's bedroom in the morning though I couldn't be sure, so many Africans, and Henry with his eye. Lots of people greeted Jojo, talked to him, an elderly English clergyman who was there passed him a note. He read it, nodded, and made a sign to the minister. It was cold and there were umbrellas and wet raincoats in corners and on backs of seats.

The meeting began.

I didn't understand a lot of what the four speakers on the stage were saying, I knew so little about South Africa that I couldn't follow what they were talking about and who were the people they mentioned. I understood that basically they were saying that the White government of South Africa had to be overthrown by what they called 'guerilla infiltration'. They talked about the African National Congress and Vorster and lots of names I'd never heard of. An African wearing dark glasses stood up from the audience and shouted and shouted.

The last speaker on the platform was an African, quite an old man. He spoke quietly for a long time, giving figures and statistics and talking a lot about a place called Robben Island.

And then he lifted both his arms into the air and kept saying My people My people as though he would weep. The hall, full of coughs and falling umbrellas and muttered talking was suddenly very quiet. And although I understood hardly anything I felt part of the quietness too.

'My people,' said the man and slowly let his arms fall to his sides.

'The struggle,' he said, 'is no longer for me. Or for most of you. It is for my children, for your children, for the children of the men of Robben Island. For those children to be free. We sit here in a hall in London on a raining Sunday afternoon. It is not our country, we are not with our people. Through the rain we see the faces of many English people telling us to go back home. Home. Home.' His voice broke on the last word. 'We are not allowed into our home. Is prison to be our only home? We have to *fight* for our home for that is the only way left to us. No one can talk again to us about the evils of violence. We must fight evil with evil, we must *dedicate* ourselves to violence if that is the way to our peace. *Fifteen million people to be free. Oh – my people.*

There was a stillness and then everybody clapped, me too, though I didn't understand what I was clapping. In the applause I thought I heard a voice behind me say he always does that my people bit very well doesn't he. I turned round but everyone was clapping and smiling. Then the English clergyman rose to his feet in the audience.

'Mr Chairman, Mr Chairman,' he cried, 'I must speak, please let me speak.' And the audience mumbled itself to coughing attention.

'Oh – Mr Chairman. I must implore you all, all of you here all listening to the sincere words of the previous speaker, who is my friend' – he gave a little nod at the African on the stage who nodded back – 'I must implore you to think what you are saying, what you are supporting. You must know that through the English rain of a Sunday afternoon you can also see the faces of Englishmen who are not saying to you Go back home, but rather We are with you, we are behind you in your fight against the excesses and greed of the White regime in South Africa. All of you know me, know that I am only one of many of your friends. But I cannot condone violence. The teaching of our Lord Jesus Christ can never allow us to fight evil with evil, violence with violence, killing with killing, violence can never *never* be justified. We *must* be patient, we . . .'

'PATIENCE!' cried the African with the dark glasses in the audience, jumping up. 'Are you teaching us patience you White old man, patience to die, patience to spend our lives in prison, patience to live like slaves like we've lived all our generations, patience is *finished* man, finished and now we're going to *kill* like they kill, KILL.'

He shouted the word over the hall and it had a kind of echo kill kill. I looked at Jojo. He seemed quite impassive, just sitting listening, not looking at the speakers. The clergyman was still standing, leaning on the seat in front of him, old and upset. He tried to go on talking.

'Oh my friend,' he said.

'Don't call me your friend,' shouted the African in dark glasses. '*I am not patient* and if you don't like that White old man I am not your friend. It is time for violence, it is time . . .'

'ORDER ORDER' shouted the chairman banging on his table and other voices raised and lowered into tense mumblings.

'The purpose of this public meeting as you know ORDER, please order, the purpose of this public meeting has been to form a resolution about the attitude of the people here at this meeting and the organizations that many of them represent, towards freedom fighters in

Southern Africa. I therefore put to this meeting the following resolution:

'"That this meeting called by the Anti-Apartheid Movement together with the African National Congress, supports the guerilla fighters in Southern Africa and will find what means are possible to support them from this country."

'All those in favour' . . . there were lots of hands raised, Jojo's hand raised, and some shouting.

'All those against,' shouted the chairman above the noise.

'No,' cried the clergyman standing up again, 'oh *no* we must not support violence. A few others raised their hands, all white. The clergyman looked distressed, he looked round the hall for a moment then picked up his umbrella and stepped over some legs of people in the same row and walked up the aisle and out a door at the back. The chairman declared the resolution carried.

The meeting was over. People stood up, greeted people across seats, put on raincoats.

'You'd better go home now baby,' said Jojo to me. 'I have to go to another meeting.'

'Can't I come can't I come?'

'No,' said Jojo, 'I'll ring you soon, come on I'll take you to the tube.'

It was still raining and the people streamed away from the hall into the road, hurrying. I heard Jojo telling an African he'd see him later.

'It was a very interesting meeting,' I said to Jojo.

'Yes,' said Jojo walking fast in the rain to the tube station.

The couple in the room next to me had a Pears Cyclopaedia. I borrowed it that evening and looked up South Africa.

South Africa, Republic of *ind. rep.*
(withdrew from Br. Commonwealth May 31 1961)
compr. provs. Cape Province, Natal, Transvaal
and O.F.S.; climate mediterranean to tropical;
vegetation evergreens in C. region, grassland
(veld) in E.; cereals, cotton, sugar, vines,
citrus fruit, sheep and cattle, ostriches, gold,
diamonds, coal, copper, tin, various mnfs.;
admin. cap. Pretoria, legislative cap. Cape Town;
a. (inc. Walvis Bay) 472,685 sq. m.; p. (1960)
15,841,128 (inc. est. 3,093,000 whites).

The rain still fell against the windows. I lay in bed thinking about Jojo. He had been – different – after the meeting. The same person but – withdrawn into himself – with a smooth mask betraying nothing instead of a face. I felt frightened, it wasn't the same person who laughed all the time and held me in his arms in bed only a few hours ago. It was something I thought I had noticed for a moment when he'd come to the pub near the Institution that night, but it went quickly and I thought I must have imagined it. But in the rain after the meeting I didn't imagine it. His face became a mask and his eyes were cold and he wasn't thinking about me anymore.

A voodoo mask I thought to myself, frightened in the dark, an African voodoo mask for black magic.

I had a call from the film studios to meet the wardrobe mistress at Oxford Circus.

'You'll need two outfits,' said the wardrobe mistress, 'have you got a nice skirt and jersey, say brown?'

'No,' I said.

'Well have you got a nice winter wool dress, say brown or grey?'

'No,' I said. Not very exciting to be Sean Connery's secretary I thought. I'd hoped for purple or red sexy dresses like in the James Bond films.

'Well, let's go into C & A as we're right here,' said the wardrobe mistress and in half an hour she'd bought me a grey skirt, a dark blue jersey, and a brown woollen shirt dress with a white collar.

'I suppose I couldn't have purple,' I whispered.

'Oh *no*,' she laughed, '*She* has all the bright colours, the set has to be built around *Her* clothes, secretaries are only background, believe me.' But she said it quite nicely and gave me a friendly pat on the shoulder.

'Now let's see, wear those shoes you've got on, nobody notices shoes in films, did you know that, not on secretaries anyway. Now, I'll take all these clothes down to Shepperton, you bring shoes and stockings when you come, Tuesday next week, isn't it? Yes, well they seem to be on schedule so I expect I'll see you then. Goodbye dear.' And she'd disappeared into a taxi.

A script arrived from the film company, marked 'with the compliments of . . .' and the part SANDRA written in red biro.

I looked through eagerly for Sandra, missed her completely the first time, went through again slowly. I found

I actually appeared four times when Sean Connery was in his office. Twice I just typed, and once I answered a phone, and once I said to him (in my Australian accent) 'Miss Williamson called and Mr Martin wants to know whether to expect you in Sydney tomorrow night.'

Sydney tomorrow night, my mind kept the words for a moment, Sydney tomorrow night, March, the heat and the cicadas at night as you fall asleep, and where we lived trams in the distance clanging bells, the heavy scent of flowers and the feeling of the sea not far away. Jojo would like it I thought, I could take him there, he'd like the heat and the sea and the smells, it must be like South Africa. Jojo. I love him. I'm in love, those cliched words everyone uses, this is what they mean when they say in love. With Alfie I felt sophistication to be living with him. And tied to him because we lived together and knew each other and were used to each other. And relied on him. And felt lonely afterwards. But never once this feeling now of – absoluteness. The gas heater went slowly out, small blue flame and then coldness and I looked for another shilling, still carrying the script that said *in Sydney tomorrow night*.

And when he called in to see me the next evening carrying books and papers and his eyes looking tired so much work to catch up that he'd missed, laughing still but in a tireder way, my love flowed over and around him, not for one moment did I think of the mask face that frightened me, or of holding back, of not saying I love you, of protecting myself from future hurt, of being proud. I loved him entirely. He seemed – not startled but surprised at the — absoluteness – of my feelings all at once but I felt such urgency to say everything, I still had the feeling that he might disappear to Dar-es-Salaam again before I'd had time to tell him how much I loved him. He listened to me, telling him; his eyes were dark and tired and beautiful and he watched me talking to him, he was sitting by the heater holding a cup of coffee and he said looking at the gas flames I won't go away without telling you.

And that night his books and his papers lay on the table and he made love to me and perhaps seemed to love me too.

I woke to find him getting dressed in the cold dark of my room.

' Where are you going?'

'Well I'd better leave before everyone wakes up and I have some work to do.'

'But it's only,' I felt for my watch, 'six o'clock, it's so early.'

'I have to go now,' he said and even in the darkness I felt the mask come down.

The film studios rang me and said I should be at Shepperton Studios at seven o'clock on Tuesday morning. They didn't say anything about a car, I thought film stars travelled in cars, I rang my agent.

'Freddie how do I get to Shepperton Studios at seven o'clock in the morning?'

'Well dear, hire a car, much the best thing, doesn't look too good arriving on the first train with all the extras when you're actually playing a part, you *must*, always, keep up appearances, I'll lend you the money if you need it, and another thing darling be sure to eat in the restaurant, try to eat with Sean Connery if you can, *lucky* you dear! then other people will look at you, notice you you know what I mean, *must* play your cards right darling, be seen by the right people bye.'

I told Jojo on the phone that I had to go to the studios in a chauffeured car to keep up appearances. I heard him laugh and laugh on the other end of the phone and then talk to someone and then I recognized Mohale's loud mad laugh, the one that used to echo sometimes round the corridors of the Institution.

'Mohale says,' said Jojo, 'you must also pretend to have a lot of money so that people will think you're rich and prosperous because you've made lots of films, so then they'll give you more film parts.'

'Oh,' I said. 'I see.'

And I could hear them both laughing.

'Come over,' said Jojo, 'and we'll take you out for a meal and teach you how to be a film star.'

We laughed so much that night across the red and white checked tablecloth in the little café we often went to, that I thought once more my heart might burst with happiness. People stared at us especially as Mohale's funny loud laugh echoed round the café, and I realized I felt proud I didn't mind people looking I felt sorry for them because they weren't having such a good time as we were, I loved Jojo so much, I was happier than I'd ever been in my life, that pain of happiness again. People stared and looked sometimes – uglily – at us, if that can describe the looks on some people's faces, tight-mouthed. Mohale kept telling more and more outrageous stories about films, about making a film in Algeria and the star being so drunk at the end of nine months' shooting that they had hired special people at special salaries to sober him up for the mornings. Jojo's arm was across the back of my chair as we talked I felt his hand dry and warm on the back of my neck. I looked at him and he smiled at me and Mohale watched us and then said to me quietly across the table,

'I told you he'd come back baby,' and he and Jojo looked at each other for a moment and then the waiter brought the coffee.

Mohale went off after the meal to meet someone and Jojo and I went for a drink. Just inside the door of the pub was a small dog and as Jojo went across to the bar I bent down to pat the dog.

'Hello,' I said to the dog. 'Hello.'

'She'd sleep with a dog if she'd sleep with a nigger.'

The voice was quite near my ear as I bent down, except that I thought I must be mistaken, that I couldn't really have heard someone say that. I stood up quite slowly and saw a man just next to me, looking at me, his face quite twisted with anger. He said nothing, just stared at me, waiting, and I stared at him. Then I walked up to the bar where Jojo was and said:

'Wasn't Mohale funny with all those stories,' and Jojo laughed and took me across to a table on the other side of the pub and put some money in the juke box and a voice called, 'Hey, Jojo,' and it was Henry with his funny eye and he came and sat with us with another African called George and we all talked and laughed together and I looked once across at the door where the man was sitting and he was watching me and I looked away and laughed very very loud like the others.

It seemed preposterous to be sitting huddled alone in the back of a car being driven through dark and empty London early in the morning with no breakfast. Out into the country, arriving at the big gates of the studio, still dark, uniformed guards waving the cars through. The studio I was directed to was a huge deserted building like an old tin aerodrome hangar, just a few unshaded lights in empty corridors and my echoing footsteps but a yawning young man appeared from the darkness to meet me.

'Good morning, I'm the third assistant, sorry we've had to call you in so early but we need you ready at a moment's notice if we get on to the office scenes this morning.'

He took me upstairs to the make-up room.

'This is the famous Augusta, she'll look after you, your dressing-room is H, I'll leave the key in the door.'

The famous Augusta was making a cup of tea from an electric kettle and reading the *Daily Mirror*. The room was warm, a transistor radio was playing 'Please Please Me' rather staticly. She made me a cup of tea too, and started putting heavy layers of rather orangey make-up on my face and idly gossiping about people whose names I'd only read in newspapers, have you met Sean Connery yet dear? Oh – a *lovely* man, you'll like him. She chattered on about the films and film stars she'd made up and who was lovely and who wasn't, of course dear you had to come early so *she* could have a sleep-in, everything revolves around *her*, close your eyes that's right dear, a mesmerizing mixture of talk and quiet pop music and the warmth and my eye make-up being applied by someone else and only 7.45 in the morning. Then to the hairdresser who put my hair into what she considered to be a secretary-like roll at the back of my neck and told me that Sean Connery was lovely. Then the third assistant appeared again, took me to my dressing-room and said we'll call you when we need you. It was twenty past eight. I heard voices outside the door which seemed to imply that *She* had arrived . . . My dressing-room had a chair and a bed and a basin and a dressing table in it. I sat there in my new C & A brown woollen dress which the wardrobe mistress had told me to put on, until 12.45. I didn't like to lie down because of my hair and my make-up and my dress, and I didn't have anything to read. I heard sounds along the corridors as though there were lots of people and then later silence, or somebody's voice calling someone and running feet and quite often the sounds of bells ringing, and then silence again. It felt like a dream, as though I'd be left there forever in the warm dressing-room, half asleep, listening for voices, waiting. Then the third assistant put his head round the door and said,

'You can go to lunch now, there's been a hold-up in the last scene, you won't be needed till at least three o'clock.'

He smiled and went away.

Lunch. I was terribly hungry with no breakfast. I walked in my make-up and my hairstyle and my brown woollen dress anxiously along corridors, down stairs, past closed doors, past people leaning on walls, past arguing voices, past a big door with a red light flashing. I saw the third assistant, my only contact with reality.

'Oh please,' I said, 'where do I get lunch?'

'Oh the restaurant,' he said, 'out the doors of the studio, turn right along to the end of the road, you can't miss it.'

Outside it was freezing cold, lots of people in strange clothes walking quickly, other studios like the one I'd come out of, lots of buildings. I came to the restaurant and walked inside into the warmth. It was crowded with people sitting at tables, all talking and laughing loudly to each other, and waving. There was lots of noise. I looked anxiously for somewhere I could sit, but there seemed to be nowhere. I advanced to what seemed to be an empty place, but it had 'Reserved' written on it. Then I looked up and saw Joan Crawford sitting at the next table. I couldn't believe my eyes. Then I looked across and saw Diana Dors sitting at another table talking to Christopher Lee. People seemed to be looking at me. I turned and fled, out into the cold and back to the studio and up the stairs and along the corridors to my dressing-room where I sat, hungry but safe, and listened again to the voices outside the door.

Towards the end of the day the third assistant came and took me downstairs into the set where they were filming. I was introduced to the director, an American, who shook my hand warmly and said 'Glad to have you with us on the picture,' and to Sean Connery who said the same. The studio was extraordinary, a much bigger version of what I'd seen on my Twickenham trip to the Beatles, lights everywhere – up in the roof, in corners, hanging from wires, cameras being pushed along with men riding on the top, and clapper-boards that were banged before each scene started just like I'd seen at the pictures. Part of an office was being put together in one corner by a lot of men, and Sean Connery and the director were reading a newspaper together in another corner and laughing. I stood uneasily, moving out of the way of cables and men in overalls, trying not to look as though I didn't belong or had no idea what would happen next.

Then I was rehearsed by the director for a scene: I had to stand by the phone, pick it up and say 'Good morning, Mr Morgan's office . . . yes . . . yes . . . just one moment I'll put you through.' That was all, that was the scene. But I had to face a certain way as I picked up the telephone, stand on a mark, move to one side of the desk as I said I'll put you through, and remember to keep my head up all the time. It was hard to remember everything, I wasn't really thinking about the character I was playing like I did on the stage.

'Um . . . What sort of a girl is she do you think?' I asked the director.

He looked surprised.

'Well, just – you know – a secretary,' he said.

'I see,' I said. So I kept thinking head up face this way move now. Then after a man had looked at me through a tube they said thank you and I was told to relax while they lit the scene. I was now almost fainting with hunger. As I watched, another girl went and stood by the desk where I had been standing and a man kept putting lighting gauges up by her face and by the telephone.

'Cup of tea love,' said a man and I nearly threw my

arms around his neck. He was the props man, Harry, and he kept explaining things to me, who people were: the grip, the clapper-boy, the stand-ins, the lighting cameraman (who didn't work the camera), the sound man who was hidden away behind the set wearing earphones and pressing lots of buttons and talking about the 3.40 at Kempton Park.

Then I was called to do my scene and found my hand shaking as I picked up the phone. The director noticed and came over to me.

'Don't worry,' he said, 'we can take it a few times if it doesn't work at first.' He didn't seem at all like film directors I had heard actors talking about in pubs, film directors who shouted and screamed and walked off the set. He just smiled and patted my shoulder.

We rehearsed it again, first I forgot to keep my head up then I forgot to move round the desk, finally I got everything right at once. Then the lighting cameraman put a lighting gauge on my face and the director called right let em roll and the second director shouted QUIET and a bell rang and a cameraman said cameras rolling and a voice from behind the set called sound rolling and a boy ran in front of the camera saying scene three hundred and three take one and clapped his board and ran away again and the director said ring the phone and the phone rang and I answered it (look left) spoke into it (keep head up) said *I'll put you through* (move around desk) cut cried the director save the bell cried the second director and the bell rang again and a drop of sweat ran from under my armpit down my side.

The director smiled at me again.

'That was fine, just fine,' he said, 'only you did look a bit scared as though the phone might blow up in your face when you answered it.'

Everyone laughed a bit and I did too. 'Let's try again,' said the director and the whole performance was repeated again, don't look scared, don't look scared, head up, I said to myself, and this time the director cried 'Cut' and 'Print it', and 'Thank you', to me and 'Arthur where's my tea,' to the third assistant and Sean Connery smiled at me and there I was a film star.

And I was a film star for four days for which I was paid £100 and the days were the same, a kind of dream world of early mornings, chauffeured cars, made-up faces and bells ringing, and long long periods of nothing to do when I sat with a newspaper in front of me and thought about Jojo. Once Harry, the props man, took me for lunch in the staff cafeteria which was next to the restaurant and where all the technical staff and extras usually ate and I had lunch with Harry and the clapper boy and an assistant cameraman from another film. When I got back from lunch that day a middle-aged actor who was playing a part about the same size as mine asked me where I ate lunch.

'I've been in the cafeteria with Harry,' I said.

He looked shocked.

'You shouldn't eat in there,' he said.

'Why?'

'People will think you're not earning much money and can't afford to eat in the restaurant.'

'Well, I'm not earning much money and anyway the restaurant's terrifying.'

'But people must *think* you're getting a lot of money, otherwise you won't get any more jobs.'

'Why?'

'Because that's how people get jobs. I'll take you in tomorrow,' he said kindly, 'if you're scared, I'll show you around.'

And the last day he shepherded me in past faces I recognized to a table against a wall and all through lunch as he talked to me his eyes flickered backwards and forwards over the people and he gave a wave and a smile when he caught the eye of people he knew.

'You see,' he said to me as we walked back to the set, 'that's the way to be seen by people and get jobs.'

Next day I was back in Westminster where old men shuffled in the doorways of the Labour Exchange and there was a funny smell.

Chapter XI

I didn't get a lot of work. I didn't stop much to think about whether it was because I wasn't very good, or not very pretty, or my legs were too skinny. I was so much in love with Jojo that everything else was secondary and I only worried about work when I simply didn't have enough money to pay the rent. Sometimes my agent lent me money, sometimes Jojo, though I found that he usually had to borrow from one of the others to lend to me. I did, twice, take a temporary typing job and the clicking sound in the offices echoed insistently in my head long after I'd gone home to Camden Town in the crowded tube. Sometimes I had an eightpenny tin of spaghetti for dinner, sometimes I had a huge steak in a restaurant with Jojo, sometimes he made porridge for breakfast. I lived more at his place than at mine, although that usually meant odd black faces popping round the door to discuss things, especially Henry who I felt vaguely didn't like me. When Jojo was at my place he felt uneasy and although the couple next door were pleasant to him, the woman downstairs told me I was disgusting and she would tell the landlord I had black men in my room. She never said anything to Jojo though, in fact I used to hear her say 'Good evening' to him as he came up the creaking stairs.

I did the occasional play for a repertory company and odd bits for television, I always seemed to be playing secretaries, I must've had that look about me or perhaps it was my typist training. I didn't mind being out of work when the sun was shining: I would go to Primrose Hill and lie down and close my eyes and think of Jojo. He was always at lectures and meetings, his final exams were coming up and he was working terribly hard. But if I hadn't seen him or heard from him for two or three days I would panic and think he had gone to Dar-es-Salaam.

We went to lots of parties, marvellous loud parties like the first one and, slowly, I learnt to dance. Now, looking back, I can't distinguish all the parties: the laughter the drinking the talking – the evenings were all the same, joyous to me, night after night of people laughing and dancing and music blaring out of rooms in streets in Kentish Town and Camden Town and Ladbroke Grove and Baker Street. There were other white girls at the parties, sometimes different ones sometimes the same. There were African girls that I came to recognize but when I said hello they were mostly cold towards me and made me feel uncomfortable.

And being with Jojo.

I used to wonder sometimes, scared, whether he wouldn't get tired of being with me if I couldn't talk to him about the things that interested him. I went back to the Westminster Reference Library and looked up books about South Africa. I tried very hard to concentrate and understand. I read about the Relief of Mafeking and General Smuts and lots of figures and tables about population and exports and it all seemed so complicated, nothing to do with Jojo laughing at a party, and in the end I'd give up and sit in the whispering library watching the black students in their suits and the old men sleeping.

I remember a time when we'd been out very late and had walked a long way home. I remember how glad I was to fall into bed in his room and Jojo gave a long sigh too as he got into bed beside me. Then after a while he said to me:

'It's all right for us. We're tired, in a comfortable bed and warm. But at home people work hard all day till they're dropping with exhaustion and they haven't got comfortable soft beds to get into. And warm rooms. Some nights when I hear rain and wind outside and feel so warm and secure in bed I feel' – he paused for quite a long time looking for a word, a habit of his – 'ashamed.' And he lay holding me, awake and thinking.

Another night when there'd been reports in the news-papers of fighting somewhere in England between English and Pakistanis and a Pakistani had been killed he said suddenly, in the middle of the night:

'It's different for us, the South Africans, we're exiles, we have to wait, but we'll go home one day, that's how we see our future. But, I'm thinking of the West Indians, the Pakistanis, the Indians, the people, well, who've come here to settle, they've – left behind their countries and their' – he kept groping for words – 'old lives. What about the people who work on buses or own shops or work in factories and hospitals who have to mix all the time with British people because that is their life forever, I wonder – what will happen to them in England, if there will be any big – outcry – one day, against them. A politician could do it.'

And he lay there thinking in the night.

I used to enjoy listening to him talking on the telephone. He'd often talk in the language I didn't understand, interspersed with little bits of English like 'mind you' and 'the stupid fellow' and 'yes yes yes' and 'you know man' all mixed up with the African language and lots of laughter and waving his hands in the air.

And there were times, the times of the mask over his face, when he was like a stranger and I learnt no way of getting through to him until he was ready to be with me again.

Once my friends in Tooting Bec had a party and I took Jojo with me. There were lots of Australians there and people got very drunk and talked about good old Aussie and the Pommies and some of them stared at Jojo who was the only black person there. It got noisier and noisier and some people started singing 'A Pub With No Beer'. Only it was a different kind of noise and singing than at the parties I'd been to with Jojo, I tried to think what the difference was as I drank some lovely Australian beer, I suppose it was a sort of – rougher – noise. I saw Jojo talking to my friend's husband, the school teacher and they seemed to be getting on well together so I relaxed a bit and drank more beer and talked to some people from home that I knew. But Louise kept coming up and telling them I was a film star and they'd feel shy no matter how much I said it wasn't true, and then they saw that I was with Jojo and that made people more strained. Not unfriendly, but curious, and that Australian unease about people getting above themselves. One Australian, Peter MacDonald, I remembered him from Sydney, he was a good surfer and his father owned a chain of chemist stores and was rich, actually said 'Hello boy' to Jojo and Jojo only smiled. Louise took me into the kitchen and started asking me about Jojo so I just said 'I love him' as it seemed to answer all her questions. But she looked incredulous.

'You mean you'd marry him?'

'Yes I would,' I said.

'But,' she looked dismayed, 'what about children, I mean it's not fair on the children, they'd be coloured, you mustn't have coloured children, I mean we live right among them out here, they're *different*, they're really different, you ask Eddie, he *knows*, he *teaches* them.'

I didn't say anything.

'I mean,' she was drinking and drinking, 'where would you live? He's a South African.'

'Well, he misses South Africa.' I drank more beer and thought of his face sometimes, talking about the beaches and the heat and the wildness. 'If we couldn't go there, he'd like Australia, it'd be like South Africa in lots of ways.'

'*Are you mad?* You *must* know about the White Australian Policy.'

'What?'

'The White Australian Policy. Only whites acceptable. You *can't* not know that at your age.'

'But that's *stupid*,' I said, 'and anyway he'd be married to me, I'm an Australian.'

She looked at me the way people sometimes looked at me, as though I hadn't quite grasped things.

'You try it,' she said and walked away from me into the other room. I ran after her.

'Louise is it true?'

'Oh God, of course it's true, you can't be *so* dumb as you seem, and anyway,' she was drunk and fell against a chair and picked herself up again, 'you can't marry a black man, it isn't right, it's peculiar.' And she stared at Jojo across the shouting back-slapping room that smelt of beer.

We caught the last tube home from Tooting Bec, Jojo and I, and some of the others all shouting and laughing and singing songs. Jojo and I sat alone at one end of the carriage.

'I'm sorry that man called you boy like that,' I said.

'They're not used to blacks that's all,' said Jojo calmly.

'Did you know about The White Australian Policy?' I asked him.

'Yes,' said Jojo.

And I remember one night. I'd had too much to drink and I'd been sick and he put me to bed, smoothing my hair back with his dry warm hand. He closed the door of his room and went downstairs. Later I woke up and he wasn't there. It was three o'clock in the morning and I fought with my panic as the alarm clock ticked loudly in the empty room. I hurried, I put on the white dressing gown and went downstairs, and then I heard Jojo's laugh from the sitting-room. A record was playing, that same sad voice floating out into the empty hall

> *Willow, weep for me*
> *Willow, weep for me*
> *Bend your branches down*
> *Along the ground and cover me . . .*

Only Jojo and Henry were in the room. They were talking and smoking, the room was full of cigarette smoke and the sad weeping voice singing. I stood by the door watching them, watching Jojo using his hands as he talked, with the long thin brown fingers and the cheap-looking ring he always wore on his right hand that had belonged to his father. My love for him overwhelmed me, suddenly, wild, and I started shaking violently. I wanted to run and throw myself at him and cry I love you I love you. But I made myself keep standing there by the door in the white dressing gown and they were engrossed, talking about South Africa and some route from Cape Town to Pretoria. So I went out into the hall and into the kitchen, still shaking, my whole body shaking. I stood there against the stove for a long time. Then I made some coffee and took it in for them to drink and they looked pleased and I sat drinking coffee with them wondering desperately if I could turn this violent feeling of love into something useful like making coffee or typing so that Jojo would love me too. For I somehow knew that the way his face lit up when he saw me bringing the coffee wasn't the way he would have looked if I'd run in and thrown my arms around him and cried my love as I'd so desperately wanted to.

And it was that night in bed that I learnt something about sex and love that nobody had ever told me and that I'd never read in any book. My love for him was so strong, so violent, that if in our making love there hadn't been any climax to reach any release from the violence of my feelings for him, I felt I would have – collapsed – died even – that my mind as well as my body would have burst from the tension of loving so much. So I cried out, Jojo, in the early morning grey light, and understood.

One day Jojo rang me and put off an arrangement and said there was some trouble and he might have to go to Dar-es-Salaam and he would ring me. That place, where he went away from me.

'But your exams are soon,' I cried.

'Yes, well, we'll see, goodbye,' said Jojo.

The end of summer days were tense for me, with foreboding, made worse because I didn't know what I was frightened of: I knew I was terrified about losing Jojo, but what was I losing him *to*, I had an agonized helpless sense of events going on in the world that I didn't know about, yet that were affecting me. I read newspapers, trying to understand.

He came again after a week, one evening up the

creaking stairs. He looked tired and – sad, something I hadn't ever seen in his face before.

'No, I'm not going to Dar-es-Salaam,' he said in answer to my anxious face.

'Couldn't you just *please*, tell me *something* about it,' I begged him, 'just so I could try to understand a bit.'

He drank coffee by the gas heater and told me that a lot of guerilla fighters of the African National Congress had been killed crossing through Rhodesia and Botswana to South Africa and that South African police were working in Rhodesia to help the Rhodesian Security Forces.

'You need to understand so much about the background that you don't know anything about,' he said. 'But Henry's brother was killed.'

He went away again soon saying he must do some studying, but he smiled at me and smoothed my hair back and said we'd go to a party on Saturday.

I was to meet Jojo at his place and I walked from Camden Town to Kentish Town in the late summer evening past all the people in summer clothes out for their Saturday night.

When I got there Jojo and Henry and some of the others who lived in the house and some others I didn't know were all sitting in Jojo's room drinking cheap red wine with the evening papers scattered over the floor. And I saw a headline: ZAMBIA BLAMED FOR AFRICAN INFILTRATORS. I wanted to say something to Henry about his brother but they all seemed a bit drunk and when I went in no one took any notice of me except Jojo made room for me on the bed and patted me on the shoulder. They were all talking and sometimes someone shouted and I kept staring at an African I had never seen before who I found out was a Rhodesian.

He seemed beside himself, I thought he must be terribly drunk, his eyes were nearly popping out of his head and after a while he started to cry. He shouted incoherently about whites and Ian Smith and my people and we black niggers and Harold Wilson. The room got darker, no one put a light on or closed the curtains so the streetlights from Kentish Town and the last light of the summer evening made a strange glow. Someone had given me a glass of wine. Henry started to talk about being in prison in South Africa and that was how I learnt about what happened to his eye. I think everyone in the room knew the story except me, he just told it again in a monologue, a story I couldn't believe of beatings and torture and electrodes, and he told it in a flat voice, no emotion. I felt suddenly sick and then suddenly frightened. I realized I was the only white person in the dark room. I could just see the whites of their eyes, their teeth, hear their voices, Henry talking flatly, the Rhodesian man crying. I felt for Jojo's hand in the dark but he was turned away from me, listening to Henry.

Fear enveloped me. I thought they are going to kill me all these black men in the dark and in a panic I jumped up and ran to the door knocking over a bottle of wine, and switched on the light. Everyone looked up blinking, surprised, and someone picked up the bottle I had knocked over. Red wine seeped into the old brown carpet.

'What's the matter, baby?' asked Jojo, standing up, concerned. I must have looked strange. They all looked at me, nine black men, the Rhodesian wiping his face with the back of his hand showing the pink palm.

'I . . .' I felt ludicrous, the room I slept in often, Jojo looking alarmed, the books everywhere, black faces staring at me, the wine glasses, the ashtrays, the loud ticking clock as they watched me. I looked at Henry.

'It was your story, I – couldn't bear it,' I said.

And for some reason they all laughed, Henry too.

'I can't bear it either,' said Henry and he sort of winked his bad eye at me grotesquely and they all laughed more.

'*Why are you laughing?*' I cried wildly and Jojo came over to me and made me sit down again.

'Haven't you noticed we always laugh?' said Henry, and laughing still he poured wine into everyone's glasses and people stood up, stretched, lit cigarettes. Then suddenly the Rhodesian jumped up, started shouting again.

'You can't win if you're black,' he shouted, 'there's just no place you can go. In Rhodesia Ian Smith takes over to keep the blacks in their place, here in England, the place we were brought up to sing "God Save The Queen" about when we were at school, and waving all those Union Jacks for the Royal tours, oh Jesus, here in England people say niggers go home and the A.N.C. gets this house for you people to stay in so you won't have the humiliation of trying to find a place to live – come and see my basement,' he said to me, 'see if you'd like to spend nights in my basement. The walls are wet and the room is seven pounds a week and to go to the lavatory you have to go out into the street and up through the

101

front door of the house, and there's no bath or hot water in the house at all, and its *full* of blacks and Henry's brother gets killed trying to liberate his own country. *That's what you whites are going to pay for,*' he shouted straight at me.

'Not you personally,' muttered Jojo to me, smiling a bit.

'Oh yes, why not?' The Rhodesian had heard. 'They don't differentiate between blacks, why should we differentiate between whites? And what are you doing,' he shouted at Jojo, 'with a white girl? Okay for a good lay maybe but what's she doing here, you're supposed to be working towards the liberation of Southern Africa from White Domination, not fucking white actresses – oh I know you're an actress, I've been told about you, well there's no room for you in this struggle, go and get fucked by a white man!' And he crashed out of the room and down the stairs and Henry and another African held on to Jojo and stopped him from following and talked to him, soothingly, in the language I didn't understand. I sat quite still on the bed and stared at some books that lay on the windowsill, read the titles to myself, *African Penguin Poetry Volume III, Economic History of England Vol. II, The Age of Mercantilism, Goldfinger, To the Finland Station, The Mask of Demetrius, History of Trade Unionism, The Chinese Economy.*

'Come on,' said Jojo, 'let's go to the party.' And I saw the mask on his face and his eyes quite stony.

That night in bed, the room still smelling faintly of wine, Jojo lay with his hands clasped behind his head.

'You know it's true,' he said.

'What the man said?'

'Yes.' He didn't say anything for a while. Then he got up and turned on the light and lit a cigarette and put on the white dressing gown and sat on the edge of the bed, looking like a prince again. When he spoke, he spoke gropingly like he always did when he was talking seriously. He told me that his father, a political prisoner, had been suffocated to death in the prison-van into which he and fifty-seven other Africans had been herded, to be sent from Durban to Cape Town. His mother left with five children had taken in washing as well as working as a servant for a white family. 'Her hands,' he kept saying, 'you should have seen her hands from being in water all the time, you should have seen my mother's hands.' One of his sisters, Rosa, had committed suicide. When she was eighteen her husband was picked up by the security police and detained without trial for ninety days. At the end of the ninety days they let him out and Rosa was waiting outside the prison gates: just as her husband came up to her, running smiling arms out, the police tapped him on the shoulder and re-arrested him and took him away. He was detained without trial for another ninety days, and when he was released Rosa was dead.

Jojo had also been detained in prison without trial. He had been beaten and tortured and told that he would end up like his old man. He told me that when he came out of prison he got to Dar-es-Salaam where he was involved with the African National Congress, whose leader was imprisoned for life on Robben Island. The African National Congress had decided that Jojo should study economics in London and be attached to the A.N.C. representatives there. He had a United Nations Scholarship and when he had finished his degree the A.N.C. would decide whether he should work in London or go back to Dar-es-Salaam.

He told me that the African National Congress was the biggest African opposition party to the white regime, they supported guerilla fighting in South Africa from their headquarters in Tanzania, they were setting up an underground network in South Africa, and were dedicated to the overthrow of the white government and the returning of the country to the fifteen million Africans.

And he told me that the Rhodesian who shouted at him and me was only saying what other South Africans had been saying, seeing us together such a lot.

'Does Mohale say it?' I remembered Mohale's singing soothing voice *he'll come back baby, don't you fret.* And smiling at us across the red checked table-cloth in the café.

'Oh, Mohale,' said Jojo, and smiled a bit. 'He doesn't worry about politics, he just wants to have a good time.'

'Do I have to go now?'

Jojo looked at me, and seemed to sigh.

'Do you understand what I've just been talking about?' he said.

'Yes I understand I understand but do I have to go now?'

'No,' said Jojo. 'No, not now.' And he sat there, smoking another cigarette, long brown fingers with the ring on his right hand.

'Jojo you won't go away again without telling me will you, to Dar-es-Salaam without telling me?'

'No,' said Jojo. 'I won't go away without telling you.'

For a long time that night he lay awake holding me in his arms and I was awake too, listening to the traffic outside the window, feeling his arms warm around me. I didn't want to think about what he'd said. I didn't want to think about South Africa. I could tell he was not asleep but I was too scared to speak in case he sent me away.

'Phone for you,' called the man next door one evening and I ran down the creaking stairs.

'Hello,' I said.

'Nigger-lover,' said a soft voice and then there was the click of a receiver being hung up in my ear.

Jojo continued to take me to meetings sometimes. Once I heard an African talk about the guerilla fighters in Southern Africa. The meeting was in another of those funny old halls which always seem dusty but aren't really. I looked at the audience. It was the same sort of audience as at all these kind of meetings: quite a few Africans, some Indians and a lot of white people, some middle-aged, some students with beards and long hair. I said to Jojo, there's usually Indians but not West Indians much. He told me that the Indians were all from South Africa not India, and that he'd very seldom seen any other non-whites at any of the meetings except South Africans and sometimes Rhodesians.

'Are the whites all South Africans except me then?'

'No, lots of British people are interested.'

'Why not any other non-whites from other countries?'

'They are too busy living their new lives in England,' he said. 'They are not really very interested in our particular struggle, they have their own.'

'What about other Africans then, from other African countries?'

'Not many,' said Jojo, 'not many of the ones in London.'

'I have just come back,' said the speaker, 'from being with some of the freedom fighters. You people are here tonight because, I presume, you support these men and would like to help them in some ways; and there *are* ways, and not always the more obvious ones of money.' He smiled. 'It is an unfortunate fact that it's often people without much money who want most to help' – and the audience laughed with him – 'but there *are* things,' he said, 'that you can do.'

'You must remember,' he said, 'that these men live in the hills and the forests, hiding, for months on end. Waiting. And planning. They often get cold at night, terribly cold. They need warm jerseys. You remember here in Britain during the war, didn't people knit for the soldiers?' The audience laughed again but he said, 'It's just the same in this war. Warm jerseys. Warm socks. And they have to drink any water they can find. So they need water-purifying tablets so that they don't get ill.

'And they get desperately sick of cold food all the time. They told me that one whole pocket of guerillas was lost because they were so tired of uncooked cold food that they sent two men into a village to get a small stove and they were eventually betrayed by the villagers who had seen the two men.'

'Betrayed by other Africans?' I whispered to Jojo.

'Yes,' he said.

'So little primus stoves are needed,' said the speaker. 'And sleeping bags to sleep in. And – do you know what? They get fantastically, dangerously, *bored* waiting in the hills. They told me that what they love to have are indoor games.' And again the audience laughed a bit – 'no, it's true, all that waiting, morale is so terribly important, perhaps indoor games are what they need most of all. Don't romanticize what's happening there: our fighters are men who get cold and hungry and sick and bored. Like all soldiers.'

Jojo and I walked home to Kentish Town.

'When you went to Dar-es-Salaam did you' – I paused, trying to choose my words carefully – 'did you see any guerillas?'

'Yes,' said Jojo.

And I felt a tight knot of fear somewhere in my stomach, the same place where I often used to feel as though I would burst from happiness.

Chapter XII

It was autumn, late October, cold fine sad days with the summer gone; Jojo's exams finished, his days now spent locked in consultation with A.N.C. officials in dusty crowded offices full of newspaper cuttings; dry leaves along the streets and the knowledge of another winter; it was autumn when I found I was pregnant.

For days I sat in tubes going nowhere, clenching my hands, reading notices about pregnancy tests and urine samples. Then one morning I put a sample in a bottle, wrapped the bottle in brown paper, and went to where one of the notices said. Two hours later I went back and a woman in a white coat gave me a card with a result on it: Positive. Then I sat on the tubes for more days wondering what to do next. I found myself at Ladbroke Grove one day, where Jojo and I sometimes came to parties. I walked and walked. There were lots of West

Indians and lots of children, brown and black, playing and running and calling, jumping in a few old leaves and kicking rubbish bins. I walked round and round, up and down streets that got greyer and dirtier and more run down and more full of black people. On one corner a notice said that Dr Meyer's surgery was open from five till seven in the evenings. It was a quarter to four. I sat in a café in Portobello Road and had a coke and felt sick. Then I walked again until five o'clock and then went to see Dr Meyer. In the waiting room there were seven people ahead of me, black and white, and a gas heater that made a funny spluttering noise, and old torn magazines.

Dr Meyer in a brown suit with dirty spots on it, wrote down my name and address, asked me why I didn't go to my local doctor, examined me, told me I was in the third month of pregnancy, charged me a pound, and told me to keep my legs closed next time.

I kept trying to think of ways to tell Jojo, but I let days slip past because I was so happy just with him, and was frightened to let the happiness go. In the night in the small room in his arms that held me so warmly and tightly I often started to tell him but at the last moment held back, wanting to keep the happiness just a little bit longer, listening to the clock tick and Jojo breathing evenly and the sounds of the night traffic.

Then one night Jojo and I came home from the pictures and lots of people were sitting downstairs drinking and talking and listening to music. Jojo and I went in and Jojo started talking about South Africa to one of his

friends and I sat with a glass of red wine and smiled at
Mohale who was dancing, slowly, with an African girl,
alone together in the middle of the room. Voices and
cigarette smoke and Jojo laughing at something, his head
back, his teeth white, then leaning forward again talking,
using his hands, the wine red in the glass I was holding,
Mohale dancing. And the sad-voiced woman slowly sang:

> Oh the days dwindle down
> To a precious few
> September, November.
> And these few precious days
> I'll spend with you
> These precious days . . .

I fainted, and when I opened my eyes I knew at once
from all the faces looking at me as Jojo picked me up that
everybody guessed. They said Are you all right? and
Would you like a drink of water? and Do you feel better?
but their black eyes stared at me and an African girl who
had been sitting there, the one I'd met in the bathroom
with my wet clothes the first night I had been in the
house, she got up and walked out of the room making
a tight hissing noise between her teeth.

Jojo took me upstairs.

'Are you pregnant?' he said.

'Yes,' I said.

'Why didn't you tell me?'

I lay on the bed, stared at the room and the books and
Jojo, then I said:

'Because I love you so much and have been so happy

with you and I knew this would change things in some way or other for ever, and I wanted to hold on to being happy for a few more days because I know lots of people never *never* feel this love and this happiness and I know I won't ever have these feelings again, not like this, for the rest of my life.' And I felt tears rolling down my cheeks and I turned away from the mask face in front of me and stared at the blurred wall. I heard the door close and Jojo's footsteps going down the stairs and the front door banged in the distance and I kept staring at the wall and the words of the sad woman's song went round and round in my head the days dwindle down September November these few precious days and I thought of everything that had been, and that happiness, and I knew it was gone.

I got up, tied my hair back with a rubber band, picked up my coat and went downstairs. Music was still playing, and when I paused at the bottom of the stairs I could hear the voices talking about Jojo and me. I understood from their voices that it would at least be more acceptable if I was *somebody*, a duchess, somebody useful; but I was an actress who hardly ever worked. It would be fatal, impossible for Jojo to marry me. They talked about him as if he was a kind of leader and they talked about him in a way that made it quite clear that he was theirs. Not mine.

Then I walked down to the front door and out into the dark. Mohale was standing there with the girl he'd been dancing with, smoking a cigarette. He put his black hand on my arm.

'Listen baby,' he said, embarrassed. 'It'll be all right.'

'Yes,' I said and walked away, walked from Jojo's place to my place and several times men called to me and whistled at me and I kept walking along, alone, in Camden Road at one o'clock in the morning, walking along.

Next morning Henry came to see me.

'I wondered,' he said, looking around the room, 'if Jojo was here. Never mind I wanted to talk to you. You're pregnant, aren't you.' He looked at me, his bad eye crooked.

'Yes,' I said.

'Do you know much about Jojo?' he said.

'I love him.'

'No no I don't mean that.' He sat on my bed and lit a cigarette. Sitting there, ugly.

'Jojo is one of the most important people in the African National Congress. He is one of the people who will be one of the leaders of our generation of Africans, when we take over South Africa he will be one of the most important people. He's only young, but everybody knows about him and – expects things from him.' I thought of people in pubs always knowing Jojo, the clergyman at the meeting passing him a note, the trips to Dar-es-Salaam, the way people – listened to him, the Rhodesian man crying, and shouting at him and shouting at me.

'Yes,' I said.

'Do you *understand* about South Africa?' said Henry. 'You sometimes seem so – removed – from conversations. Can't you imagine what it's *like* to grow up as a second class person, go in your Black entrance of the railway station, live in your Black part of the town, swim in your Black part of the beach, go to your Black church, get soaked waiting for a bus at a Black bus stop, hundreds and hundreds of people after work waiting in the rain for the buses that hardly ever come. Just down the road at the covered White bus shelter buses are arriving all the time for the few people who haven't brought their cars. If Jojo walked down the street in South Africa holding your White hand he'd be arrested under the Immorality Act, did you know that?' Henry got up and started walking around the room, agitated. 'We've both been in prison, you didn't like hearing the story about my eye when you were just on the way to a party did you? His father was suffocated to death because Africans are herded everywhere like cattle, like pigs,' he spat the word, 'by the White people that rule South Africa. We carry passes wherever we go, we are numbered, his mother and my mother were servants for White people, my mother died washing other people's underclothes. And you know about my brother. There are fifteen million people depending on people like Jojo and you can't *you have no right* to interfere with that just because you're pregnant. He can't have a wife who's a White actress who never gets any work, he *can't* be responsible for children yet, he's got too much to do, there's too many people rely on him, need him. I know he's fond of you, and he might feel he should marry you, but it would be *disaster.*'

'Yes,' I said.

'Well, what do you mean "yes" in that way?' said

Henry, exasperated. 'It doesn't mean anything the way you say "yes" like that.'

I put my hand on my stomach where I could feel a very slight swelling. I held it there and looked at Henry for a while, at his funny eye.

'No I mean yes I do understand what you're talking about. Do you want a cup of coffee?'

'No,' said Henry. 'Thank you.'

He went down the creaking stairs and I heard the door bang closed by the haberdashery shop.

All that day I sat by the gas heater, my hand resting on the swelling in my stomach. It felt small and round. I tried to think about the fifteen million Africans who needed Jojo, waiting in the rain for the buses, but I only knew that Jojo had gone away again. I thought of Henry's eye, and the torturing in prison and Jojo's arms round me in the night and the parties and the dancing and the loud music and the laughter and the sad woman singing. When it got dark I drew the curtains, switched on the light and sat by the gas heater again. The woman in the room underneath me had her television set on and all night as I sat there I caught half-sounds of Coronation Street and music and talking and finally God Save The Queen played to its last drum roll. Then the woman switched off her TV and I got into bed.

I woke suddenly in the cold darkness and didn't know who I was. I panicked and my mind fell round and round, trying to find itself, and I tried to sit up and I couldn't see anything and then I saw a gap in the curtains and the street light shining in and then I remembered that I was an Australian actress who'd been a typist, living in Camden Town. Then I remembered about Jojo and being pregnant and the fifteen million Africans. And then I remembered the guerilla fighters, cold in the night too, waiting for gifts of jerseys and indoor games.

Chapter XIII

Next morning I got up, was sick in my cold kitchen, went to a phone-box near the tube station, and rang an actress I knew to ask her how I could have an abortion. She said it was a shame I hadn't waited till after the abortion law was passed, and told me to ring another actress, who gave me a number to ring. I rang and a woman's voice asked me what I wanted. I told her who I was and who had told me to ring.

'Can Mr Anderson ring you back?' she said.

Well, I said, yes, and gave her the telephone number in the house. Then I waited in my room by the gas heater until Mr Anderson rang me, a suave voice mentioning nothing in particular, asking if I would like to come and see him at 5.30.

Baker Street tube station in the rush-hour, people hurrying and pushing down dirty escalators with evening papers, advertisements of girls in underwear, and me going to see a man about an abortion. A large block of flats near Baker Street, knock at a door on the fifth floor, a woman answering, smell of – disinfectant? – two girls leaving. Wax flowers on a centre table in the hall.

Mr Anderson was brisk and extremely personal. He had hair oil on. He examined me, asked me some questions and said Ah. Yes. Then he said:

'It will cost one hundred and fifty guineas. In cash. I can arrange it for' he consulted a book – 'not tomorrow, Friday at one o'clock, but then I am going to America for two weeks so you'd have to wait until I come back.'

'Friday please,' I said.

'Right.' And he wrote in the book. 'Don't have anything to eat after 10 p.m. Thursday,' he said, 'cash on Friday please, and somebody must come and collect you at 5.30 p.m. with a car. Your boyfriend perhaps?'

'No, no he's – gone away.'

He looked at me. 'Well, these things happen don't they? Someone else then, and cash on Friday.'

I went out past the wax flowers down in the lift and out into the cold grey evening, shivering but not with coldness.

I walked all the way to the Trafalgar Square Post Office that never closes. I made a collect call to my parents in Sydney. Their voices sounded alarmed over the ten thousand echoing miles.

'No, it's all right,' I said, 'it's just that – I want to come home. I haven't been very – successful here, if you could pay the fare I could work in an office as soon as I get home and pay it back to you.'

'When do you want to come?'

'Now,' I said. 'I mean next week when I've – you know – got everything fixed up.'

'Home for Christmas,' said my mother, and I could hear her talking to my father sounding pleased and excited, and then he came on the phone and the line wasn't very clear and his voice swam at me backwards and forwards over the distance but I heard him say he would go to the bank that morning and arrange about the fare.

'It'll be good to see you again,' he said, 'and it'll be lovely for Christmas.'

'Yes,' I said.

Next morning, Thursday, I went into my agent's office.

'Freddie, stop calls coming through for a minute.'

He looked surprised but phoned through to his secretary to take any messages.

'Freddie I'm going back to Australia.'

'Oh but *darling* . . .'

'I'm not being successful.'

'Well darling, I mean you've even done a film with Sean Connery, and that time in rep., and all those odd bits of television, you just *never know* what's round the corner, I wouldn't say unsuccessful, no . . .'

'Freddie.'

'Well, darling if that's what you want – I mean I always feel that there's a *chance*, love, always luck, one must be patient, it's a hard bad business and it's tough for women, but . . .' He twiddled with a ball-point pen and smoothed his hair and gazed out of the grimy window.

'Freddie, I need one hundred and fifty guineas, I'm pregnant I'm going to have an abortion then I'm going straight back to Australia, I can get the money from my parents and send it to you, really, within a couple of weeks, I'll say its debts I still owe here. I'll easily get a well-paid job as a typist, I'm very good at it, there's no reason for you to help me but I can't think of anyone else.'

Freddie's face went through surprise, shock, embarrassment, then a sort of sly look.

'It's that black man I suppose.'

I felt myself blushing.

'It's all right dear I've seen you with him a couple of times and I thought to myself that'll come to no good. Well dear we all have our preferences, mine doesn't really run to black men, Italians yes, even Spaniards, but not black men. Oh I know all that stuff' – he giggled a bit – 'about big penises, but I've never really liked the thought of being touched by a black, you know.'

I felt sick. Freddie's voice went on.

'Well, they come out true to form in the end, leave you to' – he giggled a bit again – 'carry the baby as it were, I mean they're not *responsible* like we are they're brought up differently.'

For the second time I had fainted and when I opened my eyes Freddie's face loomed large and white and alarmed over me. He sat me up and gave me a glass of water and walked around his small room.

'What guarantee will I have about the money?' he said. 'I mean it's a lot of money.'

I waited till the room had stopped spinning and moving

and then I walked over to his desk, slowly, and sat down in his chair. I picked up the ball-point pen and wrote the date.

> Dear Freddie,
>   Today I have borrowed 150 guineas from you for an abortion because of a black man. I am going back to Australia when it is over and if you haven't received 150 guineas within three weeks of my departure you can send this letter to my parents for whom the shock will be entirely overwhelming.

I signed the letter and stood up and handed it to him. He read it, shook his head a bit, and took out his cheque book and I looked out of the grimy window down on to Shaftesbury Avenue where the lights of the big successful theatres shone in the morning greyness.

Freddie handed me the cheque and pulled down his shirt cuffs, embarrassed, and told me to look after myself and best of luck and get in touch with him again if I ever came back to London.

'Yes,' I said.

I went and sat in Leicester Square, huddling in my coat, feeling the cheque in my pocket. Not many people there: a few old men sitting on other seats and young Italians reading Italian newspapers. Pigeons walking around. Taxis and buses and cars driving past and people hurrying across the street. I remembered after a while that it was my day for signing on the dole so I caught a bus to Westminster.

I walked down the cold street feeling ludicrous with the cheque for one hundred and fifty guineas in my pocket. There were a lot of people. A tramp stood in the doorway coughing and spitting and waiting. Some middle-aged women with bright lipstick and bags full of things talked to themselves. We all had green cards with our signing time written on them, it wasn't just actresses any more. And around the walls where posters said: 'Join the Army for a MAN'S life', old men and men that on closer inspection weren't so old, leaned and shuffled. As I stood there in the queue one asked me, mumbling, for a cigarette. I pretended I hadn't heard and then blushed with shame when a woman next to me gave him one and lit it for him. The heaters going, and the smell of unwashed people. Standing there I looked at the other women and wondered if any of them were pregnant. I could usually tell which were the actresses, there was an air of well-preservedness about them, and they were always impeccably made up. And then watching them, and listening, it began to seem to me that what had seemed like the chattering of birds, friendliness and gossip, had an air of hysteria about it. Or was it just me? I noticed how many of them wore dark glasses and smoked standing in queues. I realized we weren't just out-of-work actresses meeting our friends, gossiping, we were part of all those people waiting and shuffling. We were unemployed. And I was pregnant.

I went to a pub and had a tomato juice and a cheese sandwich and felt sick. Then I went and cashed Freddie's cheque at his bank as he'd instructed me.

'Could I have – an envelope, for the money?'

The cashier gave me one and I held it tightly in my pocket. Then into an Odeon cinema in the middle of a Western and saw it one and a half times. When I came out it was dark but it was only five o'clock. I kept walking and walking, bumping into the rush hour crowds, holding tightly to the envelope in my pocket. I found a sweet in my other pocket and unwrapped it and put it in my mouth. It seemed lonely, unwrapping a single sweet for myself and eating it alone in the rush-hour. Finally I had some spaghetti near Tottenham Court tube station and went back to Camden Town.

The woman next door heard me go into my room and called to me.

'Jojo was here, he was here most of the afternoon I think.'

She came into my room.

'He told me the haberdashery woman let him in, he was waiting for you, when I came home from work I found him just sitting there. He said he had to go to a meeting but would you go to his place and wait, he'd be home about eleven o'clock.'

She looked at me as I took off my coat making sure the envelope was still in the pocket.

'He didn't look – very well,' she said. 'His eyes looked – funny, you know, as if he was sick.'

I took off my shoes and put on my slippers and went into the kitchen.

'Would you like a cup of tea?' I said.

'No, no thanks we've just had one. Well anyway that's the message.'

'Yes,' I said.

In the night the bell rang a few times downstairs by the haberdashery shop. Nobody answered and after a while the ringing stopped. I lay staring into the darkness till I could see the shadow of the curtains, and of the wardrobe against the wall, and of the table by the window. Sometimes a car made a sound with its tyres as it went past. After a while I looked at my watch. It said twenty past three. I kept staring at the curtains and the shape of the wardrobe in the darkness. Later I heard milk bottles, and the sound of the traffic got louder and busier, and then it got lighter. I heard the man next door call goodbye to his wife as he went to work. Then I got up and knocked on their door.

She was putting on make-up and smiled at me in the mirror.

'Could you help me today?' I said. 'At 5.30, would you be finished work by then?'

'Yes, what is it?'

'Could you get a taxi and collect me from this address' – I had written it down – 'at 5.30 sharp because I am going to have an abortion.'

She sat down very suddenly on the bed.

'Is it Jojo?'

'Yes.'

'Does he know you're going to have an abortion?'

'No.'

'But you can't do that. God he looked terrible yester-day, didn't you see him?'

'No.'

'But it's his baby too, you can't do that.'

I stood by the door. 'Jojo has to be – he is – responsible – for – lots of people.'

'Oh God, do you mean he's married.'

'No.'

'Well *what* then?' She had got up from the bed and was looking at me agitated, and finishing her make-up and looking at her watch and putting on her high-heeled shoes and pulling her green coat out of the cupboard.

'Please will you come. They said someone has to come for me.'

'All right.' She put the piece of paper in her coat pocket. 'I hope to Christ you know what you're doing.' She paused as she went out the door.

'I like Jojo you know,' she said.

'Yes,' I said.

I didn't know if I was allowed to have a cup of coffee so I thought I'd better not. The house was terribly cold. I had a bath and did not look at my stomach or feel it with my hand. The bathroom was freezing and I shivered in the bath. The phone rang and rang in the empty hall.

Then I got dressed and went out quickly, anywhere, walking down streets in Camden Town, Primrose Hill, Regents Park, past the Zoo, along empty paths in the park cold and grey and ducks swimming in the canal. A boy with a school-bag, running, asked me the time and then ran on again. I had my hands in my pockets, feeling the envelope with one hundred and fifty-seven pounds ten shillings in cash.

At one o'clock I was in the lift up to the fifth floor and ringing the bell. A different woman opened it, the warmth of the central heating hit me, there was the same smell of disinfectant and the wax flowers. Mr Anderson greeted me, smiling with the white envelope in his white hands.

'Now then,' he said.

I remember: a door opening into a bedroom, taking my clothes off, an injection in my arm, a warm warm bath, a white gown, somewhere the sound of a bell ringing, lying sideways on the bed while Mr Anderson (the doctor will be here when you're asleep, best not to know who he is) with a mask over his face hauled a gas cylinder near to me put something over my face I was panicking frightened please hold my hand will you be here when I wake up yes yes breathe in panicking fighting losing . . . fighting losing winning seeing Mr Anderson bending over me, saying my name, his face disappearing Freddie's face all the black faces everyone bending over me, a bell ringing, Mr Anderson calling me again, being sick in a basin, somebody crying somewhere, Mr Anderson's face, the hair oil a bell ringing is it gone?

'Yes,' said Mr Anderson.

'Here's a cup of tea, wake up,' said Mr Anderson. 'Your friend is waiting for you.'

I drank the warm tea that tasted of sugar.

'Now get dressed,' said Mr Anderson. 'Your friend is

here waiting for you.' He watched me as I put on my clothes.

'Keep changing the sanitary towels,' he said, 'should be cleared up completely in a day or two. If you're worried you can ring me, though I'll be in America for two weeks. But – if you haemorrhage, ring an ambulance not me, get into the nearest hospital at once and tell them you've had a miscarriage. And, I need hardly say, don't mention anything, anybody else. Don't have intercourse until after you have had your next period. And I suggest efficient contraception next time,' he said, smiling. All the time he watched me as I slowly put on my clothes.

I stumbled a bit and he took my arm and helped me along a corridor into the hall with the wax flowers. The woman from next door waited looking pale in the green coat she had taken from her wardrobe, this morning was it?

'Here she is,' said Mr Anderson, 'good as new, put her to bed nice and warm and give her something nice to eat.' Two other girls and a man were standing by the wax flowers. Mr Anderson escorted us to the door.

'Thank you Mr Anderson,' I said.

'Not at all not at all, thank *you*,' said Mr Anderson and the door closed behind us.

She took my arm and we got into the lift.

'Was it awful?' she whispered.

'I can't remember much,' I whispered back. And we went out into the same cold grey day.

I fell as I was getting into the waiting, ticking taxi and she lifted me up and helped me in and put her arm around me. I lay against her shoulder and half fell asleep wondering who had been crying in another room or was it me.

Half asleep I heard the bell ringing again. I supposed Mr Anderson was there but when I opened my eyes later it was Jojo. He looked terrible. Lines of tiredness and tension in his face and his eyes were bloodshot and his pot cleaner hair had things stuck in it and he smelt of stale beer and cigarettes.

But he was staring at me.

'What's the matter with you, why are you white like that lying in bed what's happened, where have you been?'

I said: 'I've had an abortion this afternoon with gas by a man called Mr Anderson.'

He just stood there, staring at me with wild bloodshot incredulous eyes, and then I saw tears running down his brown cheeks as he stood and stared and stared. After a while I turned my face away and closed my eyes. There seemed to be voices, maybe the woman next door or maybe the television set downstairs, and doors opening and closing quietly in my dreams.

When I woke Jojo was still there, sitting by the gas heater, still staring at me. His long brown fingers stubbed out cigarette after cigarette and he still had his raincoat on and it had mud on it. He sat there, thin, like a black crow, hunched over the fire, staring at me. A stranger, I thought. I knew Alfie better.

I asked him who the sad woman was who sang those songs.

'What sad woman?' said Jojo.

'You know, I cover the waterfront I'm watching the sea will the one I love.'

'Oh,' said Jojo. 'Billie Holliday.'

Later I said: 'Jojo?'

'Yes.'

'Why did you stay with me all that time, you didn't, did you, love me?'

Jojo said, slowly: 'I think I loved you that first time I met you, you were so alone and' – fumbling for the words – 'sad, walking down that street by yourself when Mohale and I asked you to that party.'

He paused a long time, then he said, not looking at me now: 'When you got to the party and heard the music and saw all the people, you seemed to your face seemed to, light up. It was – lovely.

'And I knew it was a hopeless situation and you understood nothing about South Africa or politics, and I thought your sort of work, well, frivolous. I should have stopped seeing you a long time ago and then once I saw you one day in the Westminster Library – I could see you struggling with a book about South Africa and I just' – he shrugged – 'you seemed so, you seemed . . . to need me so much and you were – happy and you – needed me.'

'So many people,' I said, asleep, 'need – you.'

'I only left you that night to think about everything, not to leave you,' said Jojo next time I opened my eyes, fiercely, as though he had been sitting there, waiting for me to wake again.

'I was always frightened of you leaving me and going

to,' I made an effort to remember, focussing my eyes on the orange curtains, 'that place – Dar-es-Salaam.'

'Oh Jesus Christ I didn't think two days would matter, I didn't think you'd ever do anything, you didn't have the – strength, or the money' – suddenly, violent – '*where did you get the money?*'

'I borrowed it.'

'*How much?*'

I only wanted to close my eyes.

'It doesn't matter Jojo, it was my – gift – to the – guerillas,' and my eyelids felt so heavy and I was asleep.

Jojo stayed all night, hunched in his muddy raincoat by the gas fire. Once I dreamed and called out and woke, frightened, and he was there beside me holding me there baby there baby it's all right my baby don't cry. He was there on the bed holding me in his strong brown arms, my white arms tightly round his neck, my head on his shoulder, the muddy raincoat.

And then, slowly, I let my arms go and, slowly, he let go his arms and I lay back in the bed and we didn't look at each other and he pulled up the covers and went back to his chair by the heater.

In the morning when I woke again, the gas heater was out, and Jojo had gone.

In a little while the haemorrhaging started. Floods of warm blood flowing out of me and staining the sheets not hurting at all. I watched the red stains moving outwards on the whiteness, fascinated.

After a while I called the woman next door.

'Oh Christ,' she said, 'Oh Christ,' half her face made up for her office, and she ran downstairs and rang an ambulance, I heard her feet running down the creaking stairs.

They carried me down, head downwards feet up and the woman from the flat below looked out from her half-open door, I saw her staring open-mouthed, in a blue dressing gown.

In the ambulance they laid pillows under my back and the woman from next door looked terrified, sitting beside me.

'You must say you've had a miscarriage,' she whispered to me, and I heard a bell clanging along the streets.

Somebody gave me an injection and I remember being carried and wheeled along white corridors.

Doctors with masks and one of them said to me, leaning over me, putting a needle in my arm, 'who did it where did you have it done where was it.'

'I had a miscarriage.' I clung to consciousness and then there was nothing.

'Where's my baby, where's my baby' I cried, I heard my voice crying, *'where's my baby?'*

'Sssssh,' said the nurse, 'sssssh, you're disturbing the other patients.' I saw curtains around me green or purple or yellow and pain clutched at me.

It was a ward for people with lost babies and lost wombs and we read women's magazines and had mince for tea.

Chapter XIV

Heavy grey London sky and lots of planes lined up outside grounded by fog. People talking and reading and complaining and smoking and sleeping and drinking coffee and eating sandwiches and a man's newspaper saying WILSON TO ARRANGE FRESH TALKS WITH SMITH REGIME and two children running between the rows of seats falling over and laughing till their mother slapped them both.

A Christmas tree still stood in a corner, dropping pine needles, decorated with dusty coloured paper.

One telephone not being used in a row of telephone boxes.

When there weren't announcements in different languages regretting the delay there was recorded music. 'Lara's Theme' from *Dr Zhivago* sounding like cotton-wool. Then a man who was clearing paper cups started whistling the tune and made it quite jaunty. Then the sound was drowned by the next announcement as he piled used cups into a box.

'Passengers on Qantas Flight 723 to Rome, Cairo, Bahrein, Bangkok, Singapore, Perth and Sydney. Please board now at Gate Number Seven.'

I walked out across the cold windy tarmac, past a black man sweeping.

Barbara Ewing

New Zealand-born Barbara Ewing was awarded a scholarship to study drama in England at the Royal Academy of Dramatic Art, where she won the Bancroft Gold Medal. She has since acted with the Royal Shakespeare Company and in London's West End, and has appeared in many British television plays. She regularly writes her own column for the New Zealand *Listener. Strangers* is her first novel.